In Days Gone By

In Days Gone By

and Other Tales from Delmarva

Hal Roth

Nanticoke Books

Vienna, Maryland

Manufactured in the United States of America by Victor Graphics

ISBN 0-9647694-7-6

Published by Nanticoke Books, Vienna, MD 21869

For Lisa Jo,
who has always known what I am still learning:
that all life matters, supremely.

"When it's over, I want to say: all my life
I was a bride married to amazement.
I was the bridegroom, taking the world into my arms."

Mary Oliver

Illustrations

Contents

Acknowledgments

These stories first appeared in *Tidewater Times*, and I am grateful to publisher David Pulzone and editor Anne Farwell for their encouragement and the freedom they allow me to choose my subjects.

My sincere appreciation goes out to all who indulged my rabid curiosity and who shared their stories with me, often without knowing that they were contributing to a magazine feature and a book. They are Crawford Abbott, Wiley Abbott, Bertha Adams, Pat Applewhite, Claude Baynum, Everett Bradshaw, Cathy Conway, Linda Davis, the staff of the Dorchester County Library and especially Mary Handley, Beulah Dotson, Nicey Ennals, Jan Elmy, Barbara Fearson, Kathy Fisher, Nora Foxwell, Lyle Gootee, Anna Goslee, John Edward Goslee, John Groton, the staff of the Worcester County Library and especially Lisa Harrison, Tom Horton, Sharon Hurley, Granville Hurst, Christine Jews, Carroll Johnson, Jennie Johnson, Minnie Jones, Bill Keene, Jack Knowles, Billy Langfitt, Charlotte Lopus, Tom Marine, Sharon Moore, Rosie Payne, Pat Pigg, Helen Pinder, Dr. S. L. Quick, Edgar Rachall, Corbett Robbins, Dave Robbins, Evelyn Robinson, Harold Shiles, Jimmy Simmons, Myra Stanley, Ray Stokes, Roger Stone, Tracy Stone, Brice Stump, Inez Travers, a variety of Verizon employees who shall remain anonymous, Eddie Wheedleton, Mike Wheedleton, Marguerite Whilden and Howard Willey. And to those whose names I have forgotten or failed to record, I extend my apologies in addition to my gratitude.

Jo Fortier took the photograph of Lisa Jo and the Alaska Range on pages vi-vii. Images on 8, 46, 55, 152, 181, 183 and 202-203 are by photographers and artists unknown to me. The silhouette on page 152, which is the only known likeness of Paul Cuffe, is from the cover of *Black Yankees* by William D. Piersen, University of Massachusetts Press, 1988. Illustrations on 181-183 appear in *The Shannon and the Chesapeake* by H. F. Pullen, McClelland and Stewart Limited, 1970. The author took all other photographs.

And last but far from least, I want to thank Elsie Smith for reading the manuscript and for offering corrections and suggestions that were most helpful.

Introduction

This is my third collection of Delmarva tales and the first that does not contain a story about Puckum. Since publication of the "Puckum books," I am often greeted with "Oh, you're the Puckum man," and I get calls and letters almost weekly.

While volunteers from Eldorado and nearby communities were recently battling a stubborn forest fire near Puckum and Wesley Roads, my phone rang. "I thought you'd want to know that Puckum is on fire," the caller breathlessly informed me.

The tanker for Eldorado's Fire Department now bears the words "Pride of Puckum" in large, proud letters on its rear, and the company's annual Puckum Bull Roast draws a large crowd.

I still haven't discovered the origin of the name, but I continue to be advised about its location. One caller wanted me to know that her father always said Galestown was Puckum. No one had suggested Galestown before. She told me she was in her eighties, and when I asked if she knew where the name came from, she replied, "My father never said, but I'll ask some of the older folks around here." She hasn't called back.

A recent letter from Rick Bowers in South Carolina included a photograph of a road sign for "PUCKETT TOWN RD."

"I found this road not far from where I live," Bowers said. "I followed it from end to end with no evidence of Puckett Town. The only person I could find to ask said, 'Hmm, le's see. Down yonder a ways. Not too sure how far. Never been there.'"

Everybody, you see, has a Puckum.

And then there's the letter from Fred Harper (a good ol' Puckum name) in Ft. Lauderdale, Florida. Fred wrote to tell me he enjoyed the Puckum books and that he knew Sam Bull—see "The Hermit of Puckum" in *You Still Can't Get to Puckum*—when he was growing up in Hurlock. "As to finding Puckum," Fred concluded, "we never had a problem. That was because it was always right there."

So keep the calls and letters coming, all you Puckum fans, and maybe one of these days I'll write another Puckum tale. Meanwhile, I hope you will enjoy a few of these.

John Edward Goslee

Been Around and Done a Few Things

The term "jack-of-all-trades" is often tossed about lightly, but when you get to know John Goslee of Sharptown, Maryland, the label takes on a new meaning. He is not only a jack-of-all-trades; he is master of most.

As I pulled into the driveway that completely encircles his tidy, single-storied, white house, the blast of an air horn jarred me. Unsure of its point of origin or meaning, I nervously glanced about and soon spotted Goslee's ruddy, puckish grin beaming from the doorway of a small frame building. Twin horns were mounted at roof level above him on a steel pole.

This cubicle is Goslee's clock repair shop, but once it sheltered the keeper of the Sharptown drawbridge and peered down on travelers from an elevated position near the center of the span. In those days the horn squalled acknowledgment to requests from river traffic to open the pivoting center segment and permit passage.

"I did a lot of welding for them," Goslee began to explain the building's presence in his backyard, "and when they took the bridge down, they insisted I take the tenant house. I said, 'I don't want it; I got enough mess of buildings now.' But the project manager said, 'Well, you're gonna get it—if we have to come around and lay a foundation for it.' And that's just what they did. I'd been working on

1

clocks and watches in the house and I didn't have enough room, so I moved that in here."

The first grandfather clock that Goslee built still ticks the hours away in his kitchen. "People say, 'Where do you get them kits?' and I say, 'I don't have any idea. I cut the trees and saw the boards. I do the whole nine yards.'"

"Where did you learn clock making?" I asked.

"Well, I'll put it this way," he grinned. "I graduated from the University of Sharptown, and the principal's name was Professor Common Sense."

Drawing my attention back to the structure in which we had taken seats among the clutter of tools and clock parts, Goslee chuckled, "I tell people: 'You've been underneath this building many times.'

"They look at it and say, 'Blamed if I've been underneath this.'

"One woman said, 'I can't imagine what I was doing there.'"

The craftsman's ever-present grin broadened. "I told her, 'You had a man with you when I seen you.'"

Goslee's sense of humor is legendary in Sharptown and he applies it liberally whenever an opportunity presents itself. His little cocapoo is old now and hobbles about with difficulty, but the first week she came to live in the Goslee residence, her new master decided to replace the roof shingles.

"I had the ladder right to the front there, and first thing I knew, I heard something whine. That little rascal had climbed up the ladder and was on the roof with me. I was scared to death—afraid she would fall off—but it didn't bother her a bit.

"A woman come along and said, 'What kind of a dog is that?'

"I said, 'Well, it's a cocapoo, but its grandmother was a tomcat, and that's how it learned to climb.'

"She said, 'Oh, isn't that something. It amazes me how nature will pull pranks.'

"I said, 'Yeah, it does me too.'"

Although he will tell you that he grew up in his father's sawmill, one of Goslee's first jobs was working for a man named Sam Twiford, who raised watermelons and sweet potatoes along the river at the edge of Sharptown.

"My brother and some others worked for him and I wanted a job too. I went with them one Saturday morning and told old Sam I'd like to work for him.

"He said, 'What can you do?'

"I said, 'Well, most anything they can do.'

So he told them to go out and feed his old horse, and he told me: 'All right, I'm gonna try you out; I want you to sweep my kitchen floor.'

"Well, in just a few seconds I had his floor swept. He said, 'You work that fast all the time?'

"I said, 'Yes.'

"He said, 'You're hired. Go out there and tell them other SOBs they're fired.'"

Goslee's energy is another matter of legend. Dan White once wrote of him: "Goslee has one speed—all-out," but in his seventy-eighth year the five-foot-four-inch dynamo admits to slowing down a little.

One blustery March day in 1938, John Edward, as his wife and many Sharptown old timers call him, accompanied his grandfather and uncle to measure a ram schooner for a new set of sails. The *Edwin and Maude* was docked in the canal at Lewes, Delaware. "It was blowing a gale," Goslee remembers. "The man that owned her didn't know the exact length, so they had to take a tape measure and climb the mast."

His uncle was the one who usually did the climbing, but he didn't think he could make it up the slippery pole in the high wind.

"Can you go up there?" Grandfather Owens asked twelve-year-old John.

"He told me where to hold the block," Goslee explained. "He said, 'The instant you get there, touch it, and we'll have the measurement. Then drop it and come on down.'

"About the time I got up there, the wind blowed that thing so she leaned half way out in the ocean—I thought so anyway—and when she come back, if I hadn't been holding on, she'd of slingshot me clear across Lewes. But when she come straight, I slid down. I

3

burned a blister on my leg but I got it."

Years later, Goslee paid a visit to the three-masted schooner and told a companion about the climb he had made as a boy. The captain overheard the conversation and responded with a comment that he was tired of hearing all the tales people told about the boat, inferring that he didn't believe most of them.

"It kind of made me mad," Goslee said, "and I asked him, 'Have you got the log?'

"He said, 'Yes, I got the log from the day she was built.'

"I said, 'Go and get it. I can't tell you what Saturday, but it was a Saturday in March in 1938. You'll see where George G. Owens and Son measured a set of sails and delivered them in a matter of two months.'"

A little while later the captain extended an apology. "You're right," he said, "it's all there."

The *Edwin and Maude*, renamed *Victory Chimes* by the present owner, celebrated her one hundredth birthday by visiting Chesapeake Bay in the fall of 1999 and the spring of 2000. The last of her proud kind, the *Chimes* now carries passengers on cruises from her homeport in Maine.

Goslee worked in a gas station and performed light mechanic work when he was a teenager. Then, after finishing school, he was required to register for the draft, and a few months later he was ordered to report for a physical examination.

"Dr. Kuhlman had just put me in bed that same week with asthma and hay fever, and he said, 'We've got to do this, but you'll not be going nowhere.' Well, the next thing they called me to go to Baltimore, and they passed me with flying colors. In October I left to be sworn in."

Goslee recalls being transported to the train station in a 1936 Plymouth and boarding an old steam train for Baltimore. After basic training and school at Fort Riley, Kansas, he was assigned as one of the last buglers in the old horse cavalry. But the day of the army horse was done and reassignment to a mechanized unit followed quickly. The young soldier was transferred to Georgia for a few weeks and then to Massachusetts for shipment to Europe. He

4

landed on Omaha Beach six days after D-Day and joined the brutal drive across Europe with the Third Cavalry of the Third Army, under the command of General George S. Patton.

A former art teacher surprised Goslee several years ago by commissioning a portrait of him, using his photograph that appears in Dan White's *Crosscurrents in Quiet Waters* (Taylor Publishing, 1987) for a model. Along with illustrations of a shad barge, sailboat and trumpet that surround the craftsman in the painting, there are images of bronze and silver star medals. I asked for an explanation.

"Oh, I don't know," the veteran responded reluctantly. "It seems the bronze star was at Metz and Verdun."

"And the silver star?" I pressed. It is the nation's third highest medal for combat heroism.

"The war was supposed to been over," John Edward began to answer, "and we were in Austria. We were planned on leaving, but there was an uprising and they sent us to squash a bunch of German SS troopers."

In route to the encounter in the Alps, a tank in Goslee's battalion lost its brakes and rammed the back of a half-track towing an ammunition trailer, snapping the hitch and sending the trailer over a cliff. The young soldier was thrown against the back of the half-track.

"The captain carried me to thc medics," Goslee continued. "Our old doctor was drunk all the time so a staff sergeant taped me up— no x-rays or nothing." Later, Goslee would learn that he had suffered a spinal fracture.

"When we got to the place, they started shooting at us. We had six assault guns—75 MM howitzers on light tanks—and we started shelling them. After things quieted down, we went on into the town. The first thing I found was a German major. A shell had tore a chunk out of his heel. Funny thing about it, it was all gone but it wasn't even bleeding. He was an SS trooper and he was begging for something. I give him not one but two shots of morphine, and it knocked him out right good. I don't know if he made it or not.

"Then we went through town and started up a single-lane road winding around in the mountains. All of a sudden, you never heard such shooting in this world. I was in the back of a half-track and we were pinned right down. You couldn't tell where it was coming from. I got nerve enough and raised up, and I seen this German pointing one of them bazookas with a great big ball out on the end of it, aiming right down at us, ready to fire right in that half-track. I had a carbine at that time and I just stood up further and sprayed, and he come rolling down the hill. Come to find out, he was the only one shooting. He was running from behind one set of rocks to another. So that's where the other medal come in."

After the war, Goslee worked at a variety of jobs for DuPont and Criscraft and cut timber for his father's sawmill and to supply his own shop. "He can make anything out of wood," a Sharptown neighbor told me.

Goslee's greatest fame may spring from his skill as a shad barge builder. Unique to the Nanticoke River, those sleek, shallow-draw workboats have nearly disappeared since the demise of the shad industry. He launched his first barge with the help of an uncle at the age of twelve and has completed nearly two hundred boats of various design since. One of his barges is on display at the Chesapeake Bay Maritime Museum in St. Michaels. The few other survivors are scattered throughout several states. He completed his last barge in 1975, a showpiece incorporating thirteen varieties of wood.

"I sold every one I made too cheap," he told me. "I built many a one for a hundred dollars."

Goslee enjoys telling stories as much as he does building and repairing things, but he also knows how to be succinct. "What are the main steps in building a shad barge?" I asked the master boat builder.

"Start it and finish it," he replied with a smile. He has never used a set of plans.

For decades—until 1985—pulpwood was shipped from Sharptown to West Point, Virginia. Goslee worked in the wood yard for twenty-three years as operator of a floating derrick crane and yard crane, while simultaneously serving as custodian to the school in Sharptown and occasionally substituting in classes for the music or band teacher. He plays nine instruments.

A story is told about John Edward and the grand opening of the new Sharptown Bridge. He was asked to bring an antique car he had restored to the dedication and was informed that if he could round up a few additional participants, he could lead the parade. When the time came to form, a 1929 Rolls Royce pulled into the lead.

"Who's that?" Goslee asked.

"Well," the organizer explained, "Governor Schaefer is in that car. The governor is always first."

About halfway up the bridge the Rolls Royce stalled. Without a second's hesitation, Goslee pulled around it and led the parade off the bridge.

My informant tells me that the governor was scheduled to say a few words afterward but never showed up. "I guess he was pissed and went straight back to Annapolis."

The sole survivor of Sharptown's once great shipbuilding industry and his son Jimmy christened a new workboat in the fall of 2001. It may be the last wooden boat launching that Sharptown will ever witness.

And how does John Edward Goslee sum up his long and busy life? "I've been around and done a few things," he will tell you casually.

Samson Harmon

The Legend
of Samson Hat

"Samson's business was to clean and produce the mysterious hat, which he knew to be required each time he saw his master shave." Thus, George Alfred Townsend introduced one of the principal characters in his beloved novel *The Entailed Hat*.

"As soon as the lather cup and hone were agitated, Samson went, without inquiry, into a big green chest in the bedroom over the old wooden store and drew the steeple-crown out of a leather hatbox, where Meshach Milburn always sacredly replaced it himself. Then 'Samson Hat,' as the boys called him, exercised his brush vigorously and put the queer old headgear in as formal shape as possible. Periodically he attended to its rehabilitation through the medium of the village hatter, never leaving the shop until the tile had been repaired and suffering none whatever to handle it except the mechanic. In addition to this, Samson cooked his master's food and performed rough work around the store but had no other known qualification for a confidential servant except his bodily power.

"He was now old, probably sixty, but still a most formidable pugilist, and he had caught, running afoot, the last wild deer in the county. Though not a drinking man, Samson Hat never let a year pass without having a personal battle with some young, willing, and powerful Negro. His physical and mental system seemed to require some such periodical indulgence, and he measured every Negro who came to town solely in the light of his prowess. At the appearance of some Herculean or clean-chested athlete, Samson's eye would kindle, his smile start up, and his friendly salutation would be: 'You're a good man! Most as good as me!'

"Whenever Samson indulged his gladiatorial propensities, he disappeared into the forest whence he came. Being a free man of mental independence equal to his nerve, he merely waited in his lonely cabin until Meshach Milburn sent him word to return. Then silently the old Negro resumed his place, looked contrition, took the few, bitter, overbearing words of his master and brushed the ancient hat.

"Meshach kept him respectably dressed but paid him no wages. The Negro had what he wanted but wanted little. On more than one occasion the court had imposed penalties on Samson's breaches of the peace, and he lay in jail, unsolicitous and proud, until Meshach Milburn paid the fine, which he did grudgingly, for money was Meshach's sole pursuit, and he spent nothing upon himself."

The settings in Townsend's novel are real Delmarva communities, and the master journalist described them and their principal structures in such precise and accurate detail that more than a century later we can almost use his words as a regional guidebook. The same is essentially true of the book's characters, though some names have been modified for reasons known only to the author.

In Townsend's classic, Samson Hat's levelheaded approach to life and his strength and fidelity cast him as one of its principal heroes. In real life there was no "Samson Hat," but there did exist in and about the forests and towns of Worcester and Somerset Counties and at the great iron furnace on Nassawango Creek, the flesh and blood model for this fictional character, and his name was Samson Harmon.

I inquired at several libraries and museums for information about Samson Harmon and was mostly met with blank stares, but Kathy Fisher, Furnace Town's director, proved to be an enthusiastic source of information. Harmon was a long-time resident of Furnace Town, a small community nestled in the heart of the Pocomoke Forest a few miles from Snow Hill, which grew in support of the iron furnace there.

In 1788, bog ore had been discovered in the swamps along Nassawango Creek, and Maryland's General Assembly chartered the Maryland Iron Company to exploit the deposit. Commencing operations in 1832, the business was destined for abandonment within twenty years.

Ownership of the property changed hands several times before twenty-year-old Thomas Spence, who is credited with converting the furnace to the hot blast process, purchased the troubled venture. Now universally employed in the smelting of iron ore, the hot-blast method had been introduced less than ten years earlier in Scotland. Although Spence increased the production of pig iron to seven hundred tons a year, competition and the better quality of iron ore found elsewhere forced him into bankruptcy by 1850. In *The Entailed Hat,* Judge Daniel Custis is his counterpart.

The village was abandoned shortly after this culminating failure and all but the imposing brick megalith soon rotted or was carried away. By the turn of the twentieth century the humid Nassawango forest had mostly reclaimed its rightful heritage.

Sources do not agree as to how Samson Harmon came to live in Furnace Town. One proposes that Joseph Widener took him there as a slave, and when Widener moved on, Samson was freed and took up employment with the Maryland Iron Company.

Kathy Fisher surmises that Samson was the slave of Thomas Spence at the time Spence purchased the furnace and that he was freed around 1840. Before that, Samson may have belonged to Spence's father, a doctor in Snow Hill and one of the largest slave owners in the area in 1830.

The questionable account that supports Widener as having freed him claims that Samson became the personal servant of Spence when the young man purchased the furnace and that for the ensuing ten years Samson divided his time between Furnace Town and Spence's home in Princess Anne. "Wherever Spence went," the tale relates, "so went Samson, walking slightly behind the iron master."

When the business ultimately failed and Furnace Town residents moved away, Samson, having no other place to go, simply remained behind, living in an old cabin with his beloved cat, Tom. Forest neighbors brought him food and looked in on him until he could no longer take care of himself.

He was eventually removed to the almshouse in Newark, Maryland, a few miles north of Snow Hill. Samson died there in his sleep, one account claims, and although his last wish was to be buried at the furnace, he was interred, instead, at the institution. No trace remains of either the long, narrow, two-storied brick building or the cemetery nearby. The site of the graves, Fisher told me, is located next to Maryland Route 113, behind a Highway Department machine shop.

In addition to crediting Samson with sufficient swiftness afoot to run a deer to the ground, legend also claims he could catch an otter swimming in its natural element. He is said to have never worn shoes, not even in winter, and his only known photograph portrays him with bare feet.

Harmon died about 1898, somewhere in age between one hundred and six and one hundred and eight. The figure varies depending upon its source. Though Samson apparently never married, descendants of his are said to be living today in Eastern Shore communities and elsewhere.

At least five generations knew Samson Harmon, but I have discovered only two personal anecdotes that speak of him. Kathy Fisher introduced me to an unpublished manuscript titled *Stories of the Eastern Shore*. No author is cited by name in any of the ten chapters, but I was told that John S. Hill, a prominent educator from Snow Hill, had penned it.

Later, in the Worcester County Library, I learned that Hill entered his chosen profession in 1879 as the teacher at Five-Mile Branch School in Worcester County. Eventually he taught in or served as administrator to schools on both of Maryland's shores and retired after forty-five years of honorable public service. Hill was also a partner in the ownership of Peninsula Press, the state organ of the Prohibition Party, and for three years, beginning in 1879, personally edited and managed that weekly newspaper. Hill died in 1937.

In the second chapter of *Stories of the Eastern Shore*, "At the Old Furnace: The Runaway Calf and the Lost Boy," John S. Hill speaks about his "old colored friend, Uncle Samson Harmon."

"At the time I am writing of," Hill begins, "Samson was an old man, or so he seemed to me then, though he was no older than I am now.... I remember Samson used to tell me of the time when he was forty years younger and then was the 'swiftest an' strongest nigger eroun'.'

"'In dem days,' he used to say proudly, 'I c'd run down an' cotch a deer by myseff, widout help from a man er dog. I c'd whup any man dat would fight wid me, an' fro any nigger dat would rastle wid me.'

"Most people of that neighborhood believed those stories of Samson, and maybe they were true."

Hill reminisces about how desperately he had longed for a fishing rod as a boy and how he had improvised by bending a straight pin and tying it to a piece of red string. The other end of the string —which his mother had removed from a package purchased at the drugstore—was secured to a convenient switch. A horseshoe-nail sinker and a dry-stick float completed the tackle. Lifting an old board left by shingle makers had produced several worms for bait, and the young angler was off to the stream.

After eventually managing to land two minnows, the boy set out to share his accomplishment with Samson. He found the old man working in the garden.

"See, Uncle Samson, what I caught!"

"Whar on airth did yer cotch dem t'ings?"

"I didn't catch them on earth at all but in the water down by the creek, and I have a hook and line. I made it myself."

It did not require much persuasion, Hill relates, to convince Samson to accompany him. He was careful that his mother should see him with the old man, as she always felt her son to be safe when in Samson's company.

When the young angler proudly showed Samson his fishing tackle, Samson chortled, "Well, yer do beat da witches. Caught a live fish wid dat contraption, hey! Why, bless yer heart, honey. If yer'll give me dis line an' hook, I'll fix yer up as purty a rod, hook an' line as I kin make, wid a purty painted float an' a real fishhook."

Samson kept his promise and told the boy about a pond where large sunfish and what he called Roman perch could be caught. Someday, Samson said, he would take John there, but as time passed and the promise was repeatedly postponed, Hill decided to seek the fabled fishing hole on his own. "Perhaps I felt something like Columbus felt when he was setting forth on his first voyage to discover new worlds," he wrote in his memoirs.

To reach Samson's pond, the young adventurer was required to pass though an enclosure in which his father had penned a calf, but when he opened the heavy gate into the cow pasture beyond, the calf bowled him over and bounded away to join its mother. John pursued them through brush and brambles, and after running and stumbling and falling for a time, he realized that he was lost.

When the boy was missed, John's mother sent Samson to find him, a task that the old man promptly accomplished.

"I was greatly relieved by being able to get out of the thicket," said John, "but soon I began to dread the interview with my mother. Samson told me it would be all right, and here again he befriended me. He told my mother that I had wandered to the calf pasture, which I should not have done; that the calf had gotten out with the cow; that I had tried to get it back where it belonged, which also I should not have tried; but, he said, I had been in no great danger. He begged my mother not to punish me nor to worry me with more questions.

"I think now that my mother guessed the old man was concealing some things in an effort to shield me from blame, but she so honored his fidelity to me that she never afterward questioned me as to how I happened at the cow pasture that day.

"Afterwards, Samson did take me to fish in that pond several times, and I caught some fine fish there."

14

On June 8, 1885, someone with the initials J. B. wrote: "Friday afternoon we had the pleasure of visiting the furnace. The stack is still standing. The poison oak and Virginia creeper clamoring up the sides make it a thing of beauty. The mansion house...is still standing, though now falling into decay and ruin. Near it stands a log cabin occupied by...Samson Harmon, who is now one hundred and seven years old, though he looks much younger and is still well and active. We found him sitting on a handcart that was filled with firewood he had just cut. Poor old darkie! He lives there destitute of every comfort that makes life desirable—entirely forsaken and alone, except that he has the company of a cat; yet seemst [sic] to be in perfect harmony with his dready [sic] surroundings. He told us that he had raised twenty-five bushels of corn last year with the hoe. In his youthful days, as I was informed, he ran down and captured a deer, so great was his fleetness of foot. What a subject for a poem for some modern Whittier. The millpond and the old mill, the mansion in ruins and the abandoned furnace in the weird pines and the sighing cypress and the old Negro still clinging to his old cabin; all carrying us back to the days of yore when the shout of joy and the hum of industry made music in the land! Now it is the silent land, with no voices to wave the echoes save the hooting of night owls, the plaintiff cry of the whipperwill [sic] and the low crooning of the poor old Negro as he sings over to himself the melodies of the years that have forever fled."

I have heard a tale that on quiet, Furnace-Town nights, pine-filtered moonlight may reveal to the fortunate visitor the apparition of a tall black man sitting on the steps of a darkened structure or walking through the recreated village, and that by his side sits or trots a large black cat. Workers at the village sometimes do hear unusual noises at night, and they will tell you with a smile that it just may be the shuffles of an old gentleman as he wanders the grounds, calling for his cat and searching for his rightful burial place near the massive brick furnace. These are romantic visions and pleasing to the imagination, but I like the true story even better and wish I knew more of it.

Becky Phipps Cannon

Becky Phipps and the Battle of the Ice Mound

"**D**oes Becky Phipps mean anything to you?" the late Bill Keene asked me one afternoon while we were chatting in the visitors' center at Blackwater National Wildlife Refuge, where Bill and his wife, Barbara, had long served as volunteers.

"Of course," I replied. "The old cannon on Taylor's Island."

"Well," Keene offered with a sly grin, "you might say that the Becky Phipps hurled me into the world; it precipitated my coming here a little early."

The nonagenarian paused for a few seconds to allow his words to be absorbed or to measure my reaction—I couldn't tell which—then he continued: "You know Taylor's Island. As you go on the island, the property to the left is my old home—where I was born—but that's not the building. We had a one-and-a-half-story house there and my father kept store across the street. It was an old store that was standing in the war of 1812, but it's gone now.

"Those crazy bastards down there would fire that cannon every Fourth of July and New Year's Eve and election night. When they fired it on the Fourth in 1903, I was delivered a little prematurely, you might say. It scared the hell out of my poor mother, and that's pretty well the reason I have a birthday on the Fourth of July.

17

"The cannon just lay on the ground; it was too heavy for anybody to move. They used to prop it up a little but it never had a carriage. They'd take a sapling or something and shove waded paper in there. Then, on the night that Woodrow Wilson was elected, they put too much powder in it and the damn thing exploded. Part of the cannon went over the old house, and they found one piece in the creek, but they never did collect the whole thing. There's some of it missing, and that's why it's partially buried in the concrete."

When Bill and I talked, the Becky Phipps Cannon, as the war prize has come to be known, was imbedded in a base of concrete at the Taylor's Island end of the Slaughter Creek Bridge. After many years in the possession of the Spicer family, it had been placed on display there in 1950. It has since been remounted under a covered pavilion that stands in the center of a small, attractively landscaped park that also contains a Maryland historical marker and a kiosk offering a variety of free informational pamphlets.

In the late eighteenth and early nineteenth centuries, short, muzzle-loading items of ordinance such as the Becky Phipps were called carronades after Carron, Scotland, where they were first cast, and they were carried primarily on ships. The account of the capture of a British Navy tender during the last days of the War of 1812, on which this carronade was mounted, is an engaging tale that has received little attention outside Dorchester County.

It was nearly a year after their declaration of war on June 12, 1812, before the British blockaded Chesapeake Bay and brought the conflict to Eastern Shore doorsteps. In addition to cutting off isolated peninsula communities from their normal flow of commerce, parties from British ships frequently raided farms to secure provisions. Boats and property belonging to rural inhabitants were often burned, and prisoners were sometimes taken. Slaves removed from their owners' farms were shipped to British colonies such as Bermuda or held on bay islands where the king's troops were garrisoned. A few of these liberated blacks joined the Royal Navy.

Because Maryland's population was concentrated along the Chesapeake Bay and navigable tributaries, its citizens were especially vulnerable to such incursions, and individual counties responded by forming companies of militia to defend their property. For the most part these were loosely organized groups of citizens who lived at home and responded to threats that arose in their immediate neighborhood.

At the end of October, 1814, His Majesty's Ship *Dauntless* entered the Chesapeake from Halifax, its master and crew under orders to capture and destroy as many American vessels as possible and to assist in provisioning British forces on the bay.

One of the officers aboard *Dauntless* was Matthew Phibbs, who had recently received a temporary promotion from midshipman to lieutenant. Phibbs was in charge of the ship's longboat and jolly boat, described as light vessels carried at the stern of the man-of-war and utilized for boarding and securing enemy prizes.

Apparently Phibbs accomplished his assignment with expertise as the *Dauntless* log records the capture of six vessels during January, containing cargoes of stone, bottles, herrings and a goodly quantity of beer and whiskey. The *Dauntless* crew may very well have been the jolliest on Chesapeake Bay, as sailors were served a pint a day of the confiscated spirits.

On February 6, 1815, *Dauntless* was anchored off James Island, close to the mainland of Dorchester County, when its master made the following entry in the ship's log: "Saw three schooners in the Little Choptank, at dark sent longboat and jolly boat into the Choptank."

The following morning the log continues: "At day light saw ourselves surrounded with ice and by 7 o'clock the ship was fast." Then, at 8:00 that evening: "...the boats not having returned fear they are frozen in."

Joseph Fooks Stewart had grown up on his family's plantation south of Cambridge. As a slave-owning planter and operator of a shipyard, Stewart knew his livelihood was at risk, and he joined the Dorchester Militia in 1814 to help defend it. It is his report, dated February 13, 1815, on file in the National Archives in Records of the House of Representatives: Committee on Naval Affairs, that provides most of the surviving information about what transpired between February 5 and February 7, culminating in what has come to be known as the "Battle of the Ice Mound," near James Island in Dorchester County.

While the master of *Dauntless* used the terms "longboat" and "jolly boat" in the ship's log, Stewart referred to the vessels as "tender" or "schooner" and "barge" in his report.

On the evening of Sunday, February 5, Stewart informs us that a tender from *Dauntless* came near James Island and sent a barge ashore with a raiding party, whose members removed seven sheep from the farm of Moses Geohagan. When the schooner again approached the island the following evening, notice was given to Colonel Jones of the Dorchester Militia, who ordered his men to several posts in readiness and directed Stewart to distribute cartridges that had been stored in his possession.

Stewart left immediately for James Point, where he found a collection of about twenty men and boys in a position to observe the British boat. A barge was launched from the schooner at dusk, which probed the ice but failed to make landfall. After sentries had been posted to maintain a watch through the night, most of the party retired to the home of Levin Saunders, about a mile from the point.

At sunrise on Tuesday morning, February 7, the British tender lay just inside the mouth of the Little Choptank, about four hundred yards from land and trapped between the shore ice and a large cake that had drifted against her from the bay. It was the consensus of the group assembled at Saunders' that a cannon would be needed to take her, and a courier was dispatched to Cambridge to secure one.

While a majority of the militiamen then retired to their respective homes to await developments, a dissatisfied Stewart hastened back to James Point with a small band to see if more immediate action could be taken.

When he arrived at the point, Stewart observed that some loose blocks of ice had drifted into the mouth of the river and had been piled up by the action of the tide about a hundred and fifty yards from the British boat. Jumping from cake to cake to avoid the thin ice between, Stewart led his companions across the treacherous floe to this natural breastwork.

Lieutenant Phibbs and his crew had raised the tender's anchor and were loosening its sails when Stewart and his men commenced firing upon the vessel with their muskets. One of the three men on deck fell with a ball through his neck, and British weapons soon responded from the boat's hold.

Protected by their barricade of ice blocks, the Americans continued to snipe at the tender, frequently directing their shots into a sheet of canvas strung along the quarter rail, thinking that the enemy might use it as cover. After two hours the attackers' strategy proved effective, and the entire enemy party suddenly appeared on deck, waving handkerchiefs and calling for quarter.

Stewart ordered the British to leave their weapons behind and disembark. The prisoners, consisting of Lieutenant Phibbs, a midshipman, thirteen seamen, three royal marines, a black man by the name of Abraham Travers and an unnamed black woman were immediately marched ashore, and on February 10, a week before the United States Senate ratified the Treaty of Ghent to officially end the War of 1812, they were turned over to the deputy marshal for Dorchester County and transported to Easton.

In his report, Stewart listed the names of nineteen that had fought beside him at the ice mound. Nearly two centuries after the engagement, most of those surnames remain widely represented throughout the Eastern Shore: Bell, Cater, Dove, Geohagan, Hooper, North, Roberts, Simmons, Travers, Willoughby and, of course, Stewart. Only Moses Navy appears to be without a namesake today.

Wasting little time, Stewart submitted a petition to both houses of Congress on February 24, 1815, that stated in part: "Joseph Stewart...and other persons who appointed themselves under his command succeeded in Capturing a British Armed schooner at the mouth of the little Choptank river...and in making prisoners of all the persons on board.... He prays that the right of the United States, if any, to the captured vessel and public property on board of her, may be released to him and his Companions, and that they may be allowed the same bounty for each of the British Prisoners taken, as is by law granted to the owner of private armed vessels, for prisoners taken and brought in by them."

While I am unaware of any record to verify the disposition of the British boat and its contents, tradition informs us that the spoils were offered at public auction.

After the surrender of the tender's crew, a number of other citizens mingled with those who had engaged the British at the ice mound, and many of them also applied for compensation. By the time the government bureaucracy got around to making payment, the list had grown from twenty to forty-two, and the sum eventually received by Stewart on December 14, 1818, amounted to $42.90.

Although Stewart is given the rank of captain on historical markers and in Elias Jones *Revised History of Dorchester County* (1925), it must have been an honorary title. The original muster roll for Captain Thomas Wolford's detachment of Maryland's 48th Regiment of Militia of Dorchester County, which survives in the National Archives, lists him as a private and indicates that he served from April 17, 1814, to February 9, 1815.

Another report in the National Archives was written by Henry Haskins, the Deputy Marshall for Dorchester County to whom the prisoners were remanded, and confirms Stewart's rank with this statement: "I do hereby certify and make known that on the 10th February 1815, Mr. Joseph Stewart, a private in the Militia of Dorchester County, delivered to me the following British Prisoners."

So far as I have been able to determine, it is only from word-of-mouth that we know the captured black woman's name was Becky, or Becca, as it has sometimes been spelled, and that, after having been taken aboard the tender during a raid in St. Mary's County, she was serving as cook to Phibbs and his crew. While the logic may be less than clear, and I feel certain it was never intended as a compliment to anyone, the captured carronade was named in honor of her and Lieutenant Phibbs, which the passing of time has corrupted to "Phipps."

Bill Keene possessed a vast amount of historical knowledge and was a fountain of clever and amusing tales. When Bill finished his narrative of how the Becky Phipps Cannon had assisted his premature birth, he added: "I had a great grandmother who figured in the war of 1812 on Taylor's Island. Have you heard of Polly Critchett Travers? She was a Dove and married John Critchett Travers. That house at the [Slaughter Creek] bridge is where they lived.

"The limeys stole their boat one time, and the admiral who was in charge of this provisioning was Cockburn. Later he took Napoleon to his exile. John knew that if he went after the boat, they'd capture him, so my grandmother had her servant, who was also named John, row her out to the *H. M. S. Marlboro.*

"When Grandmother went aboard, the admiral came out and offered her snuff from his snuffbox, and he gave her tea. They wouldn't let her servant come in, but the admiral sent a beautiful silver platter of cake out to the boy. When John got through eating the cake, he took the platter and hid it under his seat. It was in the family for a long time, but I don't know what ever happened to it. My grandmother was a gutsy lady, and she got the boat back. The family wasn't long out of England, but they didn't like the limeys.

"After Grandmother became a little decrepit, she always took a toddy before dinner, and she would send John to the closet underneath the stairs in the hall to get her a drink. It was understood that when John went in there, he had to whistle. If he stopped whistling, she would say, 'Whistle John, whistle John.' You see John liked a little toddy too."

Believed To Be the Remains of the Polly

In Days Gone By

In Jack and Carolyn Knowles' Days Gone By Museum in Wood-land, Delaware, there is an undated manuscript of reminiscen-ces by Mary S. Handy that presents a wonderful glimpse into life on an earlier and more serene Delmarva. The text has been edited for spelling and punctuation, and the structure of some sentences and paragraphs has been slightly modified to better conform to today's standards, but the words are those of the author. The knee of an old wooden boat, believed to be from the ship Polly, which brought Mary's ancestors to Delmarva, is also on display at Days Gone By.

In the year 1783, a boat named *Polly* sailed from the islands of Bermuda to the Nanticoke River on the Eastern Shore of Mary-land. The village of Cannon's Ferry [now Woodland, Delaware] stood on this beautiful river with its woods and bluffs of sand, and it was there that the *Polly* stopped. Eight families, originally from England and Cardiff, Wales, were on the boat, including Nathaniel Bell, who is my forebear.

These people purchased land and began to farm, and each year they loaded their yield into the *Polly* and sailed back to Bermuda, where they exchanged their products for clothing, silks, sugar, cof-fee and other goods and essentials.

Broad Creek enters the Nanticoke a few miles to the south of

Cannon's Ferry, and it was there that the clan of my mother settled.

To the time of her death in her eighty-eighth year, my grandmother was fond of recalling scenes from her childhood. She had the faculty of describing them so merrily and with such fascination that I used to wish I had been born in that earlier and seemingly far more enchanting time. Her doll was only a gourd and her dishes carved from acorns, but they became, through her telling, as beautiful to me as my own china dishes and doll.

Some of my earliest recollections are of sitting around the fireside in the evening, listening to my grandmother and her friends recall the scenes and incidents of their youth. I loved to hear them speak of the "old times" and listen to stories of the Bells and other warm-hearted, jovial people of Broad Creek and surrounding districts.

My grandfather and grandmother were married in January 1844 on the old homestead. She had an unusually elaborate trousseau, consisting of a silk wedding dress.

My father's people were of Scotch ancestry, and their homestead joined that of my mother's family. Father and Mother were married in Bethel, then called Lewisville [the town's name was changed in 1850], in the old Methodist church that stood where the new one now stands. They set up housekeeping across the street from the church, and my widowed grandmother came to share the home.

The new church was built with donated lumber and money by God-fearing men and women who volunteered their labor. The preacher worked at his trade of carpentry through the week, thinking out his Sunday sermons over the saw.

My grandmother told me that while they were working on the building, Captain John Conelly would send his son Ere to our house for water for the workmen, and she would send them bread with the water. Sometimes Ere would return and say that the bread tasted so much like cake he wished he could have more.

My father was a sea captain, a business which took him away from home a great deal of the time, but it was the custom in those days to tie up the boats and spend the winter months with the family. Father was captain of the old *Merchant* and later of the *Ame-*

lia Hearn.

In those days revival meetings were held for weeks, with the church crowded until late at night. As I sat in the amen corner with my grandmother at one of those meetings, the preacher said, "Sister Bell will lead us in prayer." My grandmother answered in a clear voice: "I can't pray; I have no teeth."

My father died the year the church was finished. His was the first funeral service held there. He was a charter member of the Indian Hill Tribe of Red Men.

Whenever I think of old age (and I do think of age these days), I think of three wonderful elderly women: my grandmother, whose name I bear and who was loved by all who knew her, my mother and Aunt Julia. I think of my mother and Aunt Julia in their very stylish, tight-fitting black dresses of stiff silk with white edging, hopped back over a bustle, and their velvet bonnets, silk mitts, paisley shawls and cameo breast pins.

My grandmother has been away these many years, and my mother and aunt have also passed on, but they live for me in the pleasant halls of memory. I carry their images in my mind, and they are as clear and fresh and distinct as if I had seen them yesterday and will see them again tomorrow.

I had good parents. For me they represented everything that was true, honest and good. They had the ingrained conviction that no matter what might overtake them and their dear ones, they need fear nothing else so long as they feared God.

When I was a youngster in school, I wore the plainest clothes in the classroom, for my mother did not have the means to plan a charming wardrobe for her small daughter. Although the lack of pretty clothes seemed important for the moment, my discomfort passed. My plain clothes might have been tiresome to wear day after day, but it would have been more tiresome to lack the other things that my mother was able to give. The strength to tell the truth and never cheat in my lessons and to live up to my word of honor made my school days far more successful than any surface adornment could ever have made them.

Many times my grandmother entertained my little classmates

and myself by relating her early experiences. She would tell about the snow drifting through the chinks of the house onto the patched quilts of the beds, about the memorable journeys to visit friends at Cannon's Ferry or sailing down the Nanticoke to Sharptown, consuming almost a day in making the trip. A hundred years later, the whole state can be spanned in the time of one of those adventures.

My grandmother described her first church meetings in Quinton's schoolhouse, where they sat squeezed in the seats between the wide desks. Sometimes the wind shook the little building so hard that they thought it would go over. Sometimes the snow sifted through the cracks, and the old stove would be red to the danger point.

The preacher was a circuit rider who came from Laurel, six miles distant. One Sunday afternoon in March, Grandmother was on her way to church when she saw someone coming at break-neck speed on horseback. As the rider came nearer, she saw it was the preacher, who told her to hurry back home as there was a storm coming, and March weather was not to be depended on. He was rushing to make Laurel before the storm overtook him. Looking around, Grandmother saw only one small cloud in sight.

The same preacher called at our home later and, with a smile and twinkle in her eye, my grandmother inquired for the lady that had been waiting for him in Laurel that Sunday afternoon in March.

Another of her favorite stories was about the days before they had enough hymn books for everyone. It was the custom for the preacher to read two lines at a time for the congregation to sing. On this particular day the preacher started out by saying: "My eyes are so dim I cannot see. I left my specks at home," which the congregation sang. Then he said, "I did not give that out to sing, for that is not in the book," which they also sang.

The year when my mother was married was crowded with the making of quilts, the hemming of sheets and sewing of carpet rags. The following spring her dream of a home became a reality when they built in the town of Lewisville.

They traveled to Baltimore and bought a red and green carpet, a suite of black horsehair furniture and a marble-topped stand, which is still in my possession. They sewed the strips of carpet together and put it down over a layer of newspaper. There was the old Seth Thomas clock with the little brown church painted on the glass, a caster glass pitcher with frosted glasses, lamps with snow scenes on the globes, hand-made splashers and tidies, a cedar chest, straight-back chairs and the baby chair that was my mother's when she was a little girl, which later became mine. We had straw matting on our bedroom floors instead of carpets, which lent a special aroma to the whole house. Our yard was bordered by a bed of unpretentious, old-fashioned but sweet smelling roses on which I scratched my legs and hands and clothes.

My old home belongs to the lost loves of my life. There was an atmosphere of simplicity about it, of my mother's intelligence, her patience, her love for me and for my father, whom she mourned to the last day of her life.

I think of the days when my Aunt Julia and Uncle Glenn came to visit and we sat at the table on the back porch for dinner, of the inevitable fly-brush with its long paper streamers, which Mother and Grandmother took turns shaking over the table so that no flies would alight on the food. We always had a grand and glorious time.

I can never forget Christmas. Never since have I seen a tree look so grand. The holly tree was full of red berries and was trimmed with popcorn and butterflies of dried apples dipped in sugar. There was candy, and I can still see those red and white striped sticks that looked as big as barber poles to me.

Many times we spent Christmas at Aunt Julia's house. I remember how they pressed the gifts into our hands. I know now that Christmas was generally a time of anxiety for them, but for us it was always a wonderful experience because our loved ones were there. They could afford few gifts—my mother made most of the things out of rags and patches and love—but they gave of them-selves, that which is precious above silver and gold.

Sometimes we went to Aunt Julia's farm for the Fourth of July. Our picnic beneath the big cherry trees near the lawn consisted of ice cream and cake. It was a festive occasion.

On many summer afternoons I stood on the beautiful banks of

Broad Creek, where schooners, mud scows and fishing boats lay at anchor, watching for our ship to come in. Whenever I asked for something we could not afford, I was told that just as soon as our ship came in, I could have it.

Even allowing that money went farther in those days, I sometimes find myself pondering how my mother succeeded in keeping a comfortable roof above our heads and feeding and clothing us on the scanty income she had. We ate good food, and Mother was clever with her needle, making practically all my clothes. She was never idle from morning till night.

The house where I was born and spent my early years still stands. By no stretch of the imagination could it be termed elegant or artistic, but I think of the wonderful people that lived in that home, and it adds to my love for it. When I visit there, I have only to glance around to recall the scenes of my girlhood. Nothing can take the past away from me. Home is something besides so much lumber and plaster. We built our thoughts into the framework and planted a little of our hearts with the trees and shrubbery.

As clearly as though it was yesterday, I remember that morning in September when I first started to school. I wore a ruffled percale apron over my pink gingham dress and a pink sunbonnet. Under one arm I carried the traditional slate and pencil box. In the other hand I held a small basket that was filled to overflowing for dinner. It was my first excursion into the great world of affairs, and at the foot of the porch steps I paused to look back. My mother and grandmother stood in the doorway. My mother called me back and kissed me, and my white-haired grandmother patted my hands. As I trotted off in the direction of the building in which I was to learn that two plus two invariably equals four, I did not realize what a lovely picture those two women made then. It was not until later that I understood.

The schoolhouse sat in a clearing of timber on a hill, with pine trees and sage bushes behind it. The desks were rough shelves, four in each row, and in front were three long benches. Cloaks and bonnets were hung on nails on one side of the room. The water pail and dipper stood on a bench by the door. It was a sloppy-wet corner, except on those winter days when the dipper froze in the pail. The room was heated by a stove in the center, and we unhappily roasted or froze in proportion to our proximity to the stove.

But they were happy days. When I picture my mother and grandmother standing on the porch, I know that my life was being lived according to the rules of love. Sometimes I lie awake at night and know that somewhere they are waiting for me. My schooling will not end until my final chapter is written in the great copybook of life.

One summer afternoon, Mother and Grandmother and I sat on the porch talking lightly of things that were happening in our little town, my grandmother daring to be gay just before she took her step across the great divide. In a few days she passed away. I cannot recall her without a smile on her face and a cheery word on her tongue.

I remember once, when one of her friends came to visit, that I modestly effaced myself under the dining-room table. Her friend scooped me out with a "So this is little Mary." She placed me on her lap, wrapped her arms around me and pressed me to her bosom, then apparently forgot me while she and grandmother verbally married off and buried all the relatives over my head.

Sometimes I visit the cemetery in which most of the clan lie sleeping, just a few miles from the old homestead where they felled the first trees and turned the virgin sod: Grandfather Bell, who followed the plow; Grandmother Bell, who molded tallow candles and spun and wove; all the uncles and aunts. I think of them as a wondering child of another time. I think of the countless times that joy had joined them together on festive occasions, of when faith and trust in God had joined them together in class meetings and preaching services in the schoolhouse. Now death has drawn them together again, where they sleep on the sunny side of a sloping hill.

They Pickled
Peter Parker

It was a lovely summer afternoon. Corn, not yet tasseled, rose tall and lush, and fields of golden wheat stubble shimmered beneath an azure canopy speckled by far-ranging bands of cirrus clouds. Hardly a day for thoughts of war and violent death, but it was just that which had drawn me to the gently rolling countryside of Maryland's Kent County.

> *I sing of War, and all its thousand woes,*
> *Of bloody wounds and death's convulsive throes....*

With those words, Dr. P. Wroth began his melodramatic poem "The Battle of Caulk's Field," commemorating the only engagement fought on Eastern Shore soil during the War of 1812.

Weary of the disordered, two-year-old hostilities, Great Britain decided, in August of 1814, to initiate a decisive stroke and bring the recently independent American states to their knees. Landing on the banks of the Patuxent River with four thousand picked troops, Major General Sir Robert Ross marched on Washington. After burning Bladensburg in route, the British entered the city against minor resistance and torched the White House and Capitol along with the Navy Yard and all the vessels docked there. Then, re-boarding Vice Admiral Sir Alexander Cochrane's flotilla, they set their sights on Baltimore and its fleet of privateers that had been wreaking havoc on British merchantmen. Small groups of militia assembled across the state of Maryland and began drilling in preparation to staunch the threat.

At Bellair (now Fairlee) in Kent County, less than twenty miles directly across Chesapeake Bay from Baltimore, the Twenty-first Regiment was encamped under the command of Lieutenant Colonel Phillip A. Reed. A native of Kent County, Colonel Reed had enlisted at the age of sixteen to fight in the Revolutionary War and had risen to the rank of captain. He was now in his fifty-fourth year and had again answered his country's call to arms.

Late on Saturday afternoon, August 27, the British frigate *Menelaus*, carrying thirty-eight guns and commanded by Captain Sir Peter Parker, appeared off Kent Island with two smaller vessels. Parker was under orders from Admiral Cochrane to divert the attention of American forces in that quarter, the goal being to prevent the Kent Militia from crossing the bay to assist the defenders at Baltimore.

On Saturday night, *Menelaus* anchored off the mouth of Fairlee Creek, and on the following morning Parker led a hundred men ashore to burn every building on the Waltham farm, along with wheat in the granary and stacks still in the fields.

Two days later the Frisbee property was set to the torch, and that night *Menelaus* dropped down the bay to an anchorage off the plantation known as Chantilly. Having been informed of the whereabouts of Reed's encampment by one of Frisbee's liberated slaves, Parker was determined to surprise and capture the Kent Militia.

As an orange sun dropped from sight through summer haze that evening, Parker sat down and penned a note to his wife, who waited anxiously with their three sons for his return to England.

H. M. S. *Menelaus*,
August 30, 1814
My darling Marianne:
I am going on desperate service, and entirely depend upon

valor and example for its successful issue. If any thing befalls me, I have made a sort of will. My country will be good to you and our adored children. God Almighty bless and protect you all!

—Adieu, most beloved Marianne, Adieu!

Peter Parker

A Chestertown newspaper once quoted Parker as having said that he would eat his breakfast the following morning in Chestertown or hell, but there is no historical evidence that he ever made such a statement or intended to move on the county seat.

Dr. S. L. Quick, a resident of Fairlee and a naval architect by profession, has spent the past ten years researching and writing what he intends to be the definitive history of the War of 1812 on Chesapeake Bay. His book is entirely based upon primary sources—first-hand accounts of people who participated in or witnessed the events. Expressing embarrassment with much that has been published about the war, Dr. Quick stated emphatically to me: "I write only what the record shows. If I cannot find primary source records, it doesn't exist."

Dr. Quick is understandably protective of his research. "My references are the essence of the book," he said, "so I try not to divulge them," yet he freely discussed the Battle of Caulk's Field with me.

Sir Peter landed his contingent at the southern edge of a little tidal lake, close to where Bay Shore Road makes a sharp bend. On at least one nineteenth-century American map the spot is designated "Parker's Point," though no geographical prominence is in evidence there.

The night of August 30, we are told, was calm and hot, with a light mist crowding the bay shore. The moon had risen, and long shadows lay upon the road and fields.

Twas noon of night when round the frozen Pole
His sluggish form the Bear was seen to roll....
When hostile barges moored upon our shore,
And Albion's flag the peerless Parker bore:

34

After crossing a field between their landing site and Bay Shore Road, the British—on the advice of Frisbee's slave—marched eastward on Bay Shore to Georgetown Road. When they failed to find the Americans camped where they had been the preceding night, the march turned down Georgetown to Caulk's Field Road, where the slave knew of another favored campsite.

Colonel Reed commanded one hundred and seventy-four men divided between five companies of infantry, one of cavalry and one of artillery. About 11:30 p.m. a picket reported Parker's landing to Reed, who immediately ordered an advance down Caulk's Field Road, intent upon engaging the British, whom Reed believed had landed to burn another farm.

One hundred youths, Columbia's chosen seed,
Led on by gallant, dauntless god-like Reed;
With shining muskets gleaming from afar,
And bristly bayonets, stood the tug of war.

In route to the anticipated encounter, Reed discovered that his camp was the intended objective. I quote, in part, from the colonel's subsequent battle report to General Benjamin Chambers.

"Orders were immediately given to the Quarter Master to remove the camp and baggage, and to the troops to countermarch, pass the road [Georgetown] by the right of our camp, and form on the rising ground about three hundred paces to the rear...the left retiring on the road [Caulk's Field], the artillery in the centre, supporting the infantry on the right and left.

"I directed Captain Wickes and his Second Lieutenant Beck with a part of the rifle company to be formed so as to cover the road by which the enemy marched, and with this section I determined to post myself....

"The head of the enemy's column soon presented itself, and received the fire of our advanced party at seventy paces distant, and being pressed by numbers vastly superior, I repaired to my post on the line, having ordered the riflemen to return and form on the right of the line.

35

"The fire now became general along the whole line and was sustained by our troops with the most determined valor. The enemy pressed our front; foiled in this he threw himself upon our left flank.... Here, too, his efforts were unavailing. His fire had nearly ceased when I was informed that in some parts of our line the cartridges were entirely expended....

"Under these circumstances, I ordered the line to fall back to a convenient spot. The few remaining cartridges were distributed a-mongst a part of the line, which was again brought into the field, where it remained a considerable time, the night preventing pursuit.

"The enemy left one midshipman and eight dead men on the field and nine wounded, six of whom died in the course of a few hours.... Certain information from the enemy assures us that his total loss in killed and wounded was forty-two or forty-three...."

American casualties numbered three wounded, all of whom survived.

Although he had been instructed to remain aboard *Menelaus* after directing the troop landing, Midshipman J. T. Sands had a strong premonition that he was going to die, prompting his friends to chide him about arranging for distribution of his possessions. At the last minute, because a masters mate failed to answer the call, Commander Henry Crease ordered Sands to join the raiding party. When the Americans opened fire, Sands was struck in the chest and killed instantly by a cannon ball.

Among those who fell on the moon-drenched battleground of Caulk's Field was Sir Peter Parker, who bled to death after being wounded in the left femoral artery by a buckshot that American ri-flemen typically loaded ahead of the ball.

Out flew the ball—Sir Peter bit the ground—
Life's purple current issued from the wound!

Popular tradition contends that he was pickled in a keg of rum and returned to his beloved Marianne.

In a letter dated September 1, 1814, Commander Crease offered a deceptive version of the engagement to Admiral Cochrane. He said, in part:

"With grief the deepest, it becomes my duty to communicate the death of Sir Peter Parker, Bart., late commander of His Majesty's Ship *Menelaus* and the occurrence attending an attack on the enemy's troops on the night of the 30th....

"After a march of between four or five miles in the country we found the enemy posted on a plain surrounded by woods with the camp in their rear; they were drawn up in line and perfectly ready to receive us.... By a smart fire and instant charge we commenced the attack, forced them from their position, putting them before us in full retreat to the rear of their artillery, where they again made a stand. It was at this time while animating his men in the most heroic manner that Sir Peter Parker received his mortal wound which obliged him to quit the field and he expired in a few minutes....

"Finding it impossible to close on the enemy from the rapidity of their retreat, having pressed them upwards of a mile, I deemed it prudent to retire towards the beach...taking with us from the field twenty-five of our wounded, the whole we could find, the enemy not even attempting to regain the ground they had lost. We learnt their force amounted to five hundred militia, a troop of horse, and five pieces of artillery, and since, by flags of truce, I am led to believe their numbers much greater. Repelling a force of such magnitude with so small a body as we opposed to them, will, I trust, speak for itself, and although our loss has been severe I hope the lustre acquired to our arms will compensate for it."

Near Tolchester, the picturesque eighteenth-century Mitchell House stands hidden from travelers at the end of a long, tree-shaded lane. Now a bed and breakfast inn, the retreat is owned by Jim and Tracy Stone. Local legend holds that the British brought Sir Peter to the Mitchell House and that he died there on the kitchen table after emergency surgery failed to save his life.

"The British did not return the way they came," Mrs. Stone repeated the legend. "The route they took went past the Mitchell House and they came in for possible aid."

No report of the battle that I have seen—British or American— mentions the Mitchell House, and Dr. Quick told me: "The British

37

said they went out the same way they came in, and the description I have is that they went down Georgetown Road. I am certain Parker did not die on the kitchen table in the Mitchell House."

But Dr. Quick has found a Mitchell House connection to the Battle of Caulk's Field. "After Parker was dead, they [the British] decided to attack the Mitchell House [September 3], and they took off a Mr. Mitchell and a couple of his slaves. I discovered there was a Mr. Mitchell who was in charge of armament—guns and ammunition—for the Kent Militia. I assume it was that man, but I have not been able to make a direct connection between the two."

One of the captured Mitchell slaves—Joseph Blackwell—apparently joined the British Royal Colonial Marines and settled in Nova Scotia after the war on a ten-acre grant of land.

British casualties of the skirmish were buried along the perimeter of Caulk's Field. About 1830, Columbus A. Leary, then a young boy, returned from school one afternoon and observed a group of workmen opening a mound at the roadside. He stood and watched as the remains of Midshipman Sands were removed for return to his native England. Later, as an adult, Leary placed a stone in the hedge to mark the remaining graves. A granite monument, erected in 1902 "by Marylanders to commemorate the patriotism and fortitude of the victor and the vanquished," now marks the site.

Sir Peter slain, the hostile squadrons fled;
The woods and valleys groaned beneath their dead!
Regained their barges—plied the lab'ring oars,
And fled forever from our bloodstained shores.

Above: The Monument on Caulk's Field

Below: The Mitchell House

Delmarva's Dinosaur Fish

"**O**ld man Jim Bennett would go down to the river about sunup," the late Howard Willey once told me, "and he'd smell. If he didn't smell no sturgeon, he wouldn't put no seine on. If he did smell 'em, he'd catch four or five that day."

Years afterward, I mentioned Willey's comment to John Goslee. "That's right," the Sharptown resident responded. "When sturgeon were up here to spawn, it smelled just like a good, ripe watermelon."

Atlantic sturgeon once ranged in large numbers from Labrador to Florida. They are an ancient fish with bloodlines stretching back for at least seventy million years—perhaps a hundred and fifty million. Sturgeon swam in the waters of the earth when dinosaurs still wandered its terrain.

This enduring fish has a heavy, cylindrical body and a long, flattened and sharply V-shaped snout with four barbells on the lower jaw. It is a bottom feeder, feeling along the dark muds with its whisker-like apparatus and utilizing a specialized, tube-like mouth to suck up its fare, a diet that includes mollusks, crustaceans, worms, insects, shrimp, bottom-dwelling fish and a variety of other organisms, both alive and dead. Teeth are absent in adults. It has no true scales but is covered by five rows of bony plates called scutes. Ranging from brownish-gray to blue-black on the back and shading to white on the belly, sturgeon coloration lends itself well to a slow-moving existence along ocean and river floors.

While some believe that individuals have a potential life span of up to a hundred and fifty years, the oldest verified was sixty; and although an eighteen-foot specimen was claimed in 1842, the largest actually recorded, in 1924, was fourteen feet in length and weighed eight hundred and eleven pounds. Females reach sexual maturity between the ages of seven and thirty, when they are about seven feet long. Males mature a little earlier. Typically, fish in the northern part of their range mature later than those in the southern region. A female at Chesapeake's latitude is usually fifteen when she first spawns.

Little is known about the movements of Atlantic sturgeon in the ocean but, like shad and herring, they are anadromous, migrating in April and May into coastal estuaries and then up the rivers to spawn in currents as deep as sixty feet. Mature females reproduce once every two to six years, releasing between eight hundred thousand and four million large, sticky eggs—fewer than striped bass and shad—which scatter after being fertilized. It is estimated that less than one percent of the eggs ever develop into adults.

Within four to six weeks after spawning, females typically move downstream, while males may linger in the river or lower estuary until autumn. Juveniles are in no hurry to leave the reaches of their natal river, tarrying for as long as six years before migrating into coastal waters. While at sea, Atlantic sturgeon appear to remain close to the coast.

Perhaps attempting to rid themselves of parasites, breaching sturgeon occasionally jump clear of the water. Colonial reports are full of stories of sturgeon jumping into boats or into Indian canoes. During the Revolutionary War an American officer died of injuries sustained when a sturgeon jumped out of the Potomac River and landed on him as he was rowing across.

An early settler in the New World reported that natives would lasso a sturgeon by the tail for sport and attempt to hang on, often being pulled underwater by the flailing fish. The man who would not let go until he had exhausted the sturgeon was regarded as a brave fellow. Examination of coastal Native American fire pits has revealed numerous remains of sturgeon bones.

The fish that swam with the dinosaurs also helped to sustain the first colonists during periods of food shortages. John Smith wrote: "No place affords more plenty of sturgeon," and his claim was backed by Captain Christopher Newport in 1607, who observed that the James River "abounds with sturgeon, very large and excellent." Before tobacco captured the economic spotlight, sturgeon eggs were shipped from Jamestown to England, making caviar the first cash crop of the colony; and during the eighteenth century, sturgeon meat, eggs and oil were exported to Europe, and their air bladders were used to make a clear gelatin called isinglass, used in glue and jellies and clarifying agents.

Since colonial times the Atlantic sturgeon has supported commercial fisheries of varying magnitude. In the late 1800s it was second only to lobster among important fisheries, and landings just prior to the turn of the twentieth century were estimated at seven million pounds per year. In Chesapeake Bay the harvest of Atlantic sturgeon peaked in 1890, after which the fishery rapidly declined.

The Atlantic sturgeon is considered an excellent food fish, and its roe is a source of high quality caviar. Depending on the caviar yield, a single female has been worth between $2,000 and $4,000 to the waterman who netted it, but that hasn't always been the case. "I've heard grandfather say," John Goslee told me, "that they caught so many sturgeon it weren't nothing to catch eight to ten apiece a day, and they'd carry 'em ashore and throw 'em on the marsh— especially the bucks [males]. And there were times when the roes [females] weren't even worth it."

Sturgeon probably once spawned in every large tributary of Chesapeake Bay, but they have been decimated by overfishing, loss of habitat and water pollution, while dam construction has limited access to spawning areas. Scientists believe there is no longer a viable native Atlantic sturgeon population in the nation's largest estuary.

The Hudson River, where sturgeon flesh is known as "Albany beef," is considered to have the only vital population remaining along the East Coast, and reproduction there has fallen sharply in recent years.

The last egg-laden female sturgeon recorded in Maryland was found in the Nanticoke in 1972. The few juveniles observed in the river since then during fish surveys are thought to have migrated from elsewhere.

On the morning of July 8, 1996, a Maryland Department of Natural Resources truck loaded with large fish tanks backed up to the boat landing in Vienna on the Nanticoke River. After a few fish were dipped by net and released, large hoses sent a flood of more than three thousand year-old Atlantic sturgeon into the river. The fish, raised in the Northeast Fishery Center in Lamar, Pennsylvania, from eggs removed from Hudson River sturgeon, were each marked with a coded wire tag so they could be identified in the future. "We've got to be able to recover these fish again," warned a biologist, "or the whole program is on shaky ground." The DNR had hoped to follow up with a second stocking in October but the hatchery was unable to rear a sufficient number to warrant another release.

By early October of the following year, with rewards offered by Maryland, Virginia and the Chesapeake Bay Foundation for live recovery of any hatchery sturgeon, two hundred and sixty-two tagged fish had been recaptured throughout the Bay and as far south as the North Carolina coast. "A phenomenal return rate," beamed one Natural Resources official. "We don't expect that with any species."

The numbers recovered and the growth of individual specimens give promise that the Nanticoke and the Chesapeake still offer good habitat for this venerable species, but because of the sturgeon's delayed maturity and the infrequency of its spawning cycle, any efforts to rebuild the breeding stock must be protracted and are certain to take fifty years or more. Survivors of the first stocking are not expected to return to the Nanticoke to spawn until about 2010.

Few today have seen a sturgeon. When biologists from Pennsylvania's Lamar facility took some hatchery-raised specimens to a sports show in a Williamsport shopping center, more than two hundred thousand people stood in lines stretching from one end of the mall to the other to catch a glimpse of them. They are popular at the hatchery, too, where they swim in twenty-foot, circular tanks. "You can pat the top of the water," a biologist reported, "and they come up to you, and you can stroke them like a cow."

"The only time I was ever in a boat when a sturgeon was caught," John Goslee told me, "was right down there to Flatty Ground, just before you get to the Northwest Fork. After Dad quit pile driving, he and Harley Spear fished together. It was the last of the season and they had an old cotton shad seine that was rotten. The lines were O.K. but the net weren't no good. So what they wanted to do was lay her out and cut her out of the lines as they pulled her in. They were gonna save the line. They weren't after nothin' because it was the end of the season.

"The minute that seine got down there, Mr. Harley said, 'Eddie —my father's name was Eddie—there's a damn sturgeon out here, and what are we gonna do with that boy here?' I was about ten year old.

"Dad said, 'Catch the sturgeon; I'll take care of the boy,' and about that time it hit the blamed net.

"One of the best outboard motors I've ever seen—if it ever failed to start the first time, it was your fault—was a seven-and-a-half horsepower Elto made by old Evinrude. It was the first one to come out that had a handle to steer it with. It was heavy, cast-iron pistons and all. It had the gas tank around the fly wheel, and it was square and flat on top—plenty of room for a seat. So Dad didn't do a thing in the world but put that motor down, and he set me up on the back end of it with a five-gallon can of gas. I was scared right square to death—afraid I'd fall overboard.

"About that time the sturgeon come on top of the water, rollin'. Sometimes they just go right through the seine. But if they ease up to it and feel it on the nose, then they roll and try to get out, and they keep rollin' till they wind right up in it. When the sturgeon come up, Dad struck him across the head with a gaff—right between the eyes—and down he went a-fightin'. That old seine held him and they got him up. It weren't no time they had that thing gaffed and in the boat. It was nine foot long—big for a buck.

"The sturgeon used to be just as thick as perch on this river. The biggest one I ever seen—Harley Speer and his son Ward caught it. It was right high water on a Wednesday, at noontime, in 1938. They laid their net right out here [off Sharptown]. They got that thing in and it was exactly twelve foot long, and it had four washin' tubs of roe out of it.

"An old man by the name of Hershell Walker was out fishin' one day with a shad seine and a sturgeon got in it. He was right by hisself and had an old barge with the bottom planked lengthways. He brought the sturgeon up and got him in the boat, and while he was gettin' him in, another sturgeon came in the same net. Hershell didn't do a thing in the world but shove the sturgeon's head under the sail seat. While he was workin' on the second fish, he felt water all over his feet. That dern sturgeon had prized the bottom right off his boat. She was goin' under fast so he swum ashore. Finally, the one in the net give up and come to the top. A shad barge like that wouldn't go to the bottom; they'd go down even with the water. A bunch went out there with him and got her ashore."

Conditions in Chesapeake Bay Country have changed dramatically since sturgeon were abundant. Scientists believe that young fish can probably survive the higher temperatures and lower oxygen they will encounter in the Nanticoke and elsewhere, but spawning females need to release their eggs over hard bottoms or where grasses and debris are present to which the eggs can cling, and some spawning areas have been covered with silt in recent years. In addition, non-native species such as channel catfish and largemouth bass, which prey upon young sturgeon, are now abundant in many nursery areas. Russian biologists, who have a lot of experience with sturgeon management, tell us that catfish are probably the number one problem when stocking sturgeon fry.

Until the discovery of a dead, eight-and-a-half-foot female on the banks of the James River near Upper Brandon on October 11, 1997, the most recent clear evidence of sturgeon reproduction in the region had been in 1979.

Responding to a $100 reward for live Atlantic sturgeon, fishermen also collected about one hundred smaller specimens in the

James and neighboring rivers in 1997. One of the fish was a mere ten inches long—thought to be too small to have migrated from another river system.

In the spring of 1998 a seven-foot, eleven-inch sturgeon, described as a "potential spawner," was caught, tagged and released off Maryland's lower Eastern Shore, and a dead, egg-filled female was found off the Norfolk Naval Base. Several small fish that may have been spawned in the James River were again seen in 1998, the same year in which a petition seeking to list the Atlantic sturgeon under the Endangered Species Act was denied. "That may not prove a bad decision," a biologist remarked. "Listing them could prevent some management practices that will ultimately benefit sturgeon recovery."

At its June 1998 meeting the Atlantic States Marine Fisheries Commission closed the entire coast to sturgeon fishing for the next four decades.

Neither Heroine nor Fool

"**D**o you know the name Anna Ella Carroll?" I asked three people at random in the Maryland county where she lies at eternal rest.

"That would be the Civil War," a woman replied. "She was the lady that.... What did she do? Didn't she live in Dorchester County at one time—or something?"

"Anna Ella Carroll...? No," responded a gentleman after a moment's hesitation.

The third was quick to offer: "She was the chick who did work for Lincoln."

Often referred to as "Maryland's greatest lady" and "Lincoln's secret weapon," Anna Ella Carroll has been portrayed by some as a much-maligned heroine of American history and by others as a fraud. Citizens of her home state understand little of her life and work, and outside those boundaries she is comparatively unknown.

Born on August 29, 1815, in Somerset County, she was the eldest child of Thomas King Carroll and Julianna Stevenson Carroll. Her father was linked to two of the most distinguished families of early Maryland, the Catholic Carrolls and the Protestant Kings. The patriarch of the Carroll line was Charles, receiver of Lord Baltimore's rents from the Maryland colonists in 1691. One of his grandsons, also named Charles, signed the Declaration of Independence; and another, John, was the first Catholic archbishop in the United States.

In 1792 Colonel Henry James Carroll married Elizabeth Barnes King, daughter of Thomas King, a grandson of Presbyterian dissenter Sir Robert King, who had left Ireland in 1682 to become one of the richest planters on the Eastern Shore of Maryland. Their marriage produced three sons, including Thomas King Carroll, the eldest, who at the age of five went to live with Elizabeth's father at the family estate of Kingston Hall.

When Thomas King died shortly after the turn of the century, young Carroll was joined by his parents and brothers. He married Julianna Stevenson of Baltimore on June 23, 1814, and during the honeymoon learned of his father's death, making him heir of Kingston Hall.

Disinterested with farming, Carroll became involved in politics and took a seat in the Maryland House of Delegates the day after turning twenty-one—the youngest member ever elected. After serving as judge, he became governor for a short term in December, 1829.

In spite of his early rise to political prominence, Thomas King Carroll was not a competent man and eventually failed at every career he attempted. He was a poor manager of finances and took mortgages with improvident friends, eventually losing his slaves, horses and carriages to satisfy judgments against him. When the Panic of 1837 swept the nation, Thomas Carroll lost even Kingston Hall.

Anne, as Anna Ella was called, was then twenty-two years old. She rented a house and opened a school in an attempt to keep the family together. Conducting a girls' school was a common solution of that day for gentle women in financial difficulties. It made money, yet fell within the sphere of acceptable behavior.

In 1843 she closed the school and moved to Dorchester County, then to Baltimore in 1845 to work as a promotional writer for railroad lobbyists. By 1849, when her mother died, she was commuting between Baltimore and Washington and had begun to make the acquaintance of high ranking politicians. In 1849 she petitioned former Whig Senator John Clayton of Delaware, then Secretary of State, for a job for her father as naval officer of Baltimore. Looking for increased influence in Democratic Maryland, Clayton consented.

By the time she was thirty-five, with no husband or children to compete for her attentions, Anne was participating in the political life of the nation, and by 1850 she had become a skillful writer and lobbyist with close ties to those wielding national power. Never one to waste time with the chain of command, when she wanted something, she went straight to the top.

After the breakup of the Whigs in the 1850s, Carroll joined the American or "Know Nothing" Party and became a supporter of Millard Fillmore, who had acceded to the presidency upon the death of Zachary Taylor. Now she entered the most productive period of her career, writing books, pamphlets, editorials and articles, and articulating the party's platform in a work titled *The Great American Battle.*

She clearly delighted in being the center of political attention, but she also worked very hard. She was a lusty, liberated, twentieth century woman who had to suffer living in the nineteenth. Though petite and capable of humility, Anne became aggressive and tenacious—some say ruthless—when pursuing a goal. She tended to see issues in black and white, and when she had determined a course of action, one acquaintance claimed, she assumed that her judgments coincided with those of God. Her pride was easily and frequently wounded. In one letter to President Fillmore she wrote, "My complaint is that you can't see me as I do you—I am *great* in my womanly sphere."

The failure of most of her papers and letters to survive is a significant loss to history that is partially explained in a statement she made after a difficult situation in which a confidential letter of Fillmore's was used publicly. "Sorry I am that I trusted to anyone the letters to a mortal, and the reason I destroyed most of them was that I am not able to keep letters secure in traveling. I burn my own father's."

A cache of more than fifty of Carroll's letters written to Fillmore was discovered in 1970, and they have helped more than anything else to place her into context as a valid historical figure instead of just a legend. They substantiate the fact that she indeed had an amazing career. But her letters are full of self-importance and indignation over what she considers to be slights against her.

She once invited Fillmore to call on her. He declined, and she later wrote that she had been waiting for the opportunity to "publicly (sic) resent" what she termed his unpardonable insults. "I do not," she said in the letter, "associate you with politics anymore, but I should be forgetful of what is due myself, if I allowed any man on earth, to treat me, with such an incivility. Thank heaven, I have been more than blessed, and can earn the bread of independence, fearing God and therefore, not fearing to say of any man, what I please. With my years, I may say, under the Divine blessing, my strength has increased, and I hope yet to be a power in this land. I am in correspondence etc. with the best and first men of the Country, not one of whom but, would feel *more* than indignant upon the statement of the facts, which causes this note, but for which I will be avenged, and that before long."

In the same letter she remarked: "Now I apprise you, that, whatever is severe of you, which shall pass into history, will have its origins in your incapability to appreciate the friendship of a true woman."

Fillmore immediately responded that he had intended no disrespect but had simply been very busy. "Whatever may be your opinion of me," he wrote, "I shall ever rejoice in your prosperity and fame."

As the American Party faded from power and Fillmore was defeated by Democrat James Buchannan in 1856, Carroll, always aware of and responsive to the shifting sands of politics, turned to the Republicans.

Frantically she searched for the man who would next be president, rallying support for several in turn. When Lincoln received the nomination, she was shocked. Who was Lincoln? Carroll retreated to Church Creek to sort things out. While there, her sister Julianna and another close friend died, and Anne suffered from illness and despair for several weeks following.

But her own self-interest, coupled with a driving passion to preserve the Union, soon brought her back to Washington, where she divided her time between the crisis in national politics and maintaining Maryland in the Union. Secessionist sentiment was strong at home and she successfully urged Governor Hicks to stand firm against it, supporting his actions with a barrage of letters to newspapers.

By 1861 Carroll was writing nationally in support of Lincoln's frequently criticized policies, providing some of the best-argued rationales for his actions and making no apology for a woman's intrusion into the political arena.

Carroll boasted that she could see Lincoln on a moment's notice, but the extent of her access to the president and the degree to which she influenced his actions will never be known. There are instances where Lincoln reflected arguments Carroll made to him in letters, but only a single personal communication from the president survives, in which he thanks her for an address she made to the people of Maryland.

It was Carroll's life-long contention that while in St. Louis in the fall of 1861 she saw the folly of the Union offensive along the Mississippi, and that upon her return to Washington she conferred with Lincoln's administration, persuading them to shift the operation to the valley of the Tennessee. This change in strategy did occur and took the Confederacy by surprise, opening the way for an invasion of Georgia, control of the Mississippi and ultimately victory. She always felt that the army resented her intervention because she was a civilian and a woman and therefore, although they accepted her plan, refused to give her the recognition she deserved. In an interview later in her life she quoted Lincoln as having said: "The officers would throw off their epaulets if they knew they were acting on the plan of a civilian; and good God, if they knew it was a woman, the whole army would disband!"

The quote attributed to Lincoln is surely poetical, and many historians believe that the military was preparing to invade the South by the Tennessee and Cumberland rivers all along, but they fail to explain why such action was not taken in 1861, before Carroll's November 30 proposal to the War Department?

Though her contributions were largely rejected, she continued to propose military strategy and write for the war effort. In September, 1862, Carroll was paid $750 compensation for her service.

Carroll became concerned about Lincoln's policies, being especially annoyed at his failure to accept her council regarding emancipation, which she opposed. She attended both political conventions in 1864 and loosely supported the Democratic candidate, George B. McClellan, who had been relieved of his military command by Lincoln.

Dissatisfied with the payment she had received, Carroll took her case to Congress after the war, asking for monetary compensation comparable to a major general's salary. She received the backing of Edwin Stanton, Lincoln's secretary of war, as well as his assistant, Thomas Scott, some members of Congress and others.

Letters said to have been written by Ohio Senator Benjamin Wade include statements that would seem to remove all doubt regarding the legitimacy of Carroll's claims. "I cannot take leave of public office without expressing my deep sense of your services to the country during the whole period of our national troubles," one letter reads. "With your powerful pen you defended the cause of the Union as ably and effectively as it has ever yet been defended. From my position on the Committee of The Conduct of the War I know that some of the most successful expeditions of the war were suggested by you, among which I might instance the expedition up the Tennessee River. If ever there was a righteous claim on earth, you have one." Another letter to the Committee of Military Affairs claims that Lincoln had told him that the merit of the Tennessee Plan was due to Miss Carroll.

The published hearings of Wade's committee, however, show nothing to suggest that it ever dealt with the strategy of the Tennessee campaign. Moreover, the senator's wife was a close personal friend of Carroll's, and communications with the senator went through her. At least one of Wade's letters, which was published after his death, is almost certainly a forgery.

The Senate Committee on Military Affairs eventually approved her claim, but lawmakers repeatedly failed to vote an appropriation.

Carroll lived the final dozen years of her life partially paralyzed by a stroke and mostly in great financial distress. She rallied for a time after being stricken with pneumonia and a second stroke in the summer of 1893, but she succumbed to old age and Bright's disease during the ensuing winter.

Anna Ella Carroll—if vain and self-promotional—was a brilliant, articulate and politically informed woman who, at a time when her sex was not permitted to vote, exerted a remarkable degree of influence at the highest levels of government; yet due to a lack of corroborating evidence to support all of her claims, some would deny her any place in history.

One of the worst of current offenders may be William C. Davis, who, in an article titled "Tall Tales of the Civil War," refers to her as a nuisance, a shameless name-dropper, megalomaniac, charlatan, crackpot and obviously unstable person, who was guilty of willful misrepresentation and pure bunk, while rooted in her own self delusion, opportunism and instability. I suggest that Mr. Davis, at best, may be as egocentric as the object of his criticism and more interested in dispensing expletives than in discovering the truth.

On the serene, shaded grounds of Dorchester's Old Trinity Church, a cluster of Carroll graves begins twenty feet from one corner of the chapel. Near the center of this plot stands a short, stout obelisk bearing the following inscription on its side facing Church Creek: "Anna Ella Carroll, daughter of Thomas King and Julianna Stevenson Carroll, born at Kingston Hall, August 29, 1815, died at Washington D. C., February 19, 1893." Beneath the statistics is engraved what may be the only indisputable summary of her life: "A woman rarely gifted. An able and accomplished writer."

Carroll biographer Janet Coryell reports that Anne actually died on February 19, 1894—perhaps a fitting irony, Coryell muses, for a woman who spent much of her life trying to set her record straight. My copy of Encyclopedia Britannica claims yet a third date of February 18, 1894.

At the creek-side end of the row of monuments stands another gravestone erected by the Daughters of the American Revolution. It repeats the date on the obelisk and bears this fanciful epitaph: "Anna Ella Carroll, Maryland's Most Distinguished Lady. A great humanitarian and close friend of Abraham Lincoln. She conceived the successful Tennessee Campaign and guided the President on his Constitutional War Powers."

Anne Carroll was in many respects a truly remarkable individual, but one who embodied many contradictions. She was a southern woman, yet a unionist. She hated slavery but did not support emancipation. A prominent citizen of a state founded on principals of religious toleration, she was virulently anti-Catholic. While fighting Victorian conventions for freedoms a century before their time, she was, some say, in her business dealings, a swindler, a fraud and a cheat. Her life was far more complicated than her legend, and though she was a wide-ranging public figure, we remain unable to prove either her own grand claims or those of her detractors.

"We want no Joans of Arc," Carroll once wrote. "We want faithful and true women...who are neither heroines nor fools, American women who can stand in their own shoes."

Whatever else you choose to believe about Anna Ella Carroll, that she was, and that she did.

Anna Ella Carroll

Nanticoke Manor House

Tales of
the Manor House

I believe that most would agree with me that the Nanticoke Manor House overlooks the best landscape the town of Vienna has to offer. From its heavily planked front door a visitor can gaze down the length of Water Street, past several eighteenth-century homes that stand little more than a stone's throw from the sweeping tides of the river; and its east porch commands a panoramic view that extends from above the Route 50 bridge to where the Nanticoke bends toward Barren Creek, then twists again on its serpentine journey to Tangier Sound. The scene instills in me an enormous sense of peace and tranquility.

Captain James Kendall Lewis is said to have been a gentleman of distinct taste and wealth, and he must have shared my feelings for the spot when he settled there in 1861. The rear, frame section of the dwelling was probably constructed in the seventeen hundreds, but Lewis added the three-story brick edifice, which he declared would be "something the damned Yankees can't burn."

Captain Lewis was the owner of a fleet of sailing vessels and earned his fortune in shipping as well as in farming. He was socially prominent in the region and outspoken in his sympathy for the Southern cause. It is believed that he engaged in smuggling goods to the Confederacy, probably through a then busy facility located several miles to the south of Vienna, owned by relatives and known as Lewis Wharf to this day.

The late Susan Hitch once told Brice Stump that she well remembered an incident connected to the Manor House in the late 1800s, when the Steven B. LeCompte family resided there. In his book, *It Happened In Dorchester* (1969), Stump reported that Stella, the LeCompte's oldest child, fell deeply in love with a Frenchman named Meaupou, who ran a slaughterhouse in Vienna. Because the girl was only sixteen at the time and her suitor was old enough to be her father, the young woman's parents expressed strong objections to the affair.

When she could not be found one evening, it was learned that Miss LeCompte had made plans to meet Meaupou at a secret rendezvous. Young men with romantic interests in the maid were plentiful in Vienna, and Stella's father had no difficulty in quickly forming a search party. As the would-be beaus set off in search of the damsel, Mr. LeCompte went to Meaupou's residence and took possession of the Frenchman's horse as ransom for his daughter's return. The search party is reported to have found the young lady hiding under a bridge on the Cambridge-Vienna road and forcibly returned her, whereupon her father locked her in a third-story bedroom.

It was a long way to the ground, but ivy vines, according to Hitch, once climbed the height of the structure. Under cover of darkness, Stella is said to have utilized them to make her way to the porch roof; then she slid down a pillar and ran to her lover.

After a hastily arranged marriage, the newlyweds are reported to have made their home on the corner of Church and Middle Streets, a block from the Manor House. Miss Hitch claimed that no couple ever meant more to each other, and gradually the LeComptes came to accept their son-in-law.

Standing in front of the Manor House today, one has difficulty envisioning a sixteen-year-old girl making her way from the third floor to the ground, even with the help of ivy vines, which no longer adorn the walls. Some would dismiss the story of Stella and Meaupou as just another legend, but is it?

Older residents of Vienna refer to the property at Church and Middle as the Noble House, after the family that resided there for much of the twentieth century. David Warfield currently holds the deed and is in the process of an extensive renovation. Among documents in Warfield's possession is one that names Arthur Meaupou and R. Estella Meaupou as former owners, and family genealogical records inform us that Estella Meaupou's maiden name was LeCompte and that everyone called her "Stella."

After the LeCompte family left the Manor House, Mary Percy became its owner and later bequeathed it to her daughter-in-law. For many years it was divided into apartments and rented to several families. Then, after standing unoccupied for ten years, the landmark was purchased in 1977 by Bill and Barbara Fearson of Baltimore.

"When we first bought it," Barbara told me, "we came down to camp out for a week. The house was a wreck; plaster ceilings had fallen down and there were broken water pipes. We had an eleven-year-old dog named Loris that was part German shepherd and part collie. He lived outside a lot and just loved to come in the house. We brought Loris with us, and he was terrified. We had to drag him inside, and he just stood in the hallway shaking. He was so scared that he peed on the floor.

"Whenever Loris was in the house, he would stare and move his head like he was following something. The hair on the back of his neck would stand up and he would growl. I'd strain my eyes but I never could see anything. He scared me, and I got to the point where I didn't like staying there by myself. When we began coming down every weekend and taking extra time off, we didn't bring the dog anymore.

"A lot of strange things happened in the beginning. The doors upstairs would slam shut, and it was in the wintertime when there were no windows open to create a draft. The water in the kitchen would suddenly come on, like somebody turned a spigot.

"I was upstairs cleaning one of the bedrooms one time and I felt like I bumped into somebody. I turned around, thinking Bill had come in, but I was in the room by myself.

"I had an old spinning wheel made of cherry-wood, and it would spin all by itself. Bill had a magnetized can opener that he kept on the refrigerator, and sometimes it would spin by itself. I was like the dog; I was ready to stay in Baltimore.

"I guess I'm more superstitious or suspicious than Bill. He always had an explanation for things that happened. When the water turned on, he would say that I didn't turn it all the way off. When things moved, he would say, 'Oh well, the floor is bouncy.'

"We were sitting on an old couch one evening—Bill and I—and our son was laying on the floor in a sleeping bag. I was looking at wallpaper samples and they were watching TV. Suddenly, Bill jumped up and said, 'The TV's moving!'

"The TV was on a portable stand and I heard the wheels squeaking. I looked at my son and his head was under the sleeping bag. I started to cry and said to Bill: 'I told you things were happening around here, and you wouldn't believe me.' That night we all slept together in the same bed.

"I never felt threatened—like I was going to be hurt—or I wouldn't have come back, but I *was* scared. I didn't go upstairs alone.

"I worked for Western Electric in Baltimore for many years, and we had an engineer there who investigated poltergeists and things like that. I told him about the house and he and a couple of his friends came down and spent the weekend, hoping something would happen.

"There is an archway in the cellar that supports the internal chimneys. The kitchen has one also. The engineer brought some sort of detector with a needle on it that would move when it found energy. He found some around the chimney supports—just there and nowhere else in the house—so he took a photograph. On the second day the needle on the detector didn't move, and he took another photograph. There was a silhouette in the first picture, but in the second one it was gone. To me the image looked like a slave with her head wrapped up in a turban. It had a nose, the shape of a body and everything.

"All of this went on for about six months back in 1978, and then it stopped. I thought that whatever it was had decided we were there to stay and gave up."

Mrs. Percy communicated stories to Barbara about Captain Lewis and his wife, Mary. The couple, Percy claimed, had a son named Stephen, whom the captain favored above all else. She said Mary was restricted to her kitchen and one small room on the third floor. "I was told that he was very mean to Mary," Barbara offered.

According to Percy, the captain left the property to Stephen, bestowing only a cow and the use of the kitchen and single small room to Mary. Stephen is said to have soon lost the house in a poker game, an act that forced his mother into a home for the elderly.

Historical evidence, however, indicates that upon his death in 1868, Captain Lewis bequeathed the Manor House and $15,000—a considerable amount of money at the time—to his wife "for all her natural life and no longer."

When the Fearsons opened an inn and restaurant in the Manor House, their ghost became Mary.

"I was talking to some guests about our ghost once," Barbara said, "and when we joked about Captain Lewis, a section of plaster fell from the kitchen ceiling onto the floor. They got a big kick out of that.

"The New York Chamber of Commerce called one time and asked if we had a room available for a couple. We were the only bed and breakfast in the county at that time. I said, 'Sure, send them down.'

"Guests from New York can be difficult. I was dusting and straightening up when I looked out and saw them arrive. They were in their mid-fifties and I thought, 'Well, they look O.K.'

"I invited them into the living room and the lady immediately walked away from me and went into the second parlor. She stood in front of the fireplace and started spinning and waving her arms in the air. She stuck her hands straight out and waved them around. I looked at her husband, but he just stood there with his arms folded.

"Suddenly, the goose bumps raised up on my arms and I looked over to see if the back door was unhooked. I was planning my escape.

"She finally stopped and looked at me. It was the only time she made eye contact. She said, 'Ma'am, I'm not going to be able to stay in this house; I'm getting bad vibes.' And they left."

When we ended our chat, Barbara suggested that I talk to Sharon Hurley, who had assisted with guests at the inn and was also a waitress in the restaurant.

I briefly reviewed Barbara's stories with Sharon and asked if she knew of any others.

"Only the ones I was allowed to make up about Mary," she smiled. "I used to tell the guests that the ghost was Mary and she had come back for her room. They loved to hear about Mary. The little bedroom upstairs has the most charm of either room in the house, and I liked to sit in there and look out over the water. I got in the habit of calling it Mary's room.

"I made up a story about Mary's room. It was the smallest room and the only one the captain would let her have. I told the guests that he was the original male chauvinist pig. The women loved that. But he was fooled because the chimney makes it the warmest room in the house. I would show them where Mary sat on the steps to watch for her husband to come home. One woman really got into it. 'Oh,' she said, 'I believe I can actually see her sitting there, that poor depressed woman.'

"I loved it, and I never once ran across somebody that was afraid, but most of the time Barbara would whisper to me: 'Wait till after they get ready to leave.'"

Then Sharon's face grew serious and she said, "But this is not made up. I had to work there one Halloween night. The guests were due about eight o'clock, and just before that I went upstairs to the third floor to make sure the room was all right. When I started back down and reached the second-floor landing, it suddenly got real cold, like a window was open. I walked right into it. It felt cold and clammy and wet. I stood there and the cold just wrapped right around me. I looked at the windows, but none of them were open. When I started down again, I walked directly out of it. At the bottom of the stairs I stopped right dead and got goose bumps."

Sharon visibly shuddered. "I've got goose bumps right now, just thinking about it.

"And then I said, 'Now why?' I walked back up and the cold was gone. It was gone! I could not take myself back into that room and retrace my steps, so downstairs I went and waited for the guests. That was amazing to me.

"There is a presence in the house, and to my notion it's not bad. It's a very calm, a very serene presence. There's more to that house than people realize. No house can exist for that long and have that many people live in it without leaving a mark."

The current owners of the Nanticoke Manor House are Patrick and Deborah Kenny. And how do they feel about the ghost?

"I think Mary likes us," Debbie said with the knowing smile of someone who enjoys a good tale. "She has been very kind to us."

The Outlaws

"What people don't understand," the veteran waterman offered, his dark eyes flashing beneath the visor of a weathered baseball cap, "if'n I leave them arsters out there on the bar, they're gonna die from disease or somebody else gonna take 'em and buy shoes for their kids. Them arsters ain't worth nothin' to nobody out there on the bottom. The only way any arster or fish or crab's any good to me is when he's in my boat, and that's just the plain truth of it. God put 'em there, and I got just as much right to 'em as anybody else."

Over a beer in the Nanticoke Inn one evening a native shoreman told me that marine police once referred to the river's watermen as the meanest bunch of outlaws on Chesapeake Bay, and then he named a few.

Someone added that after repeated evasive maneuvers by one of these renegades in a fast boat, a Department of Natural Resources officer had opened fire on him from the old drawbridge at Vienna.

Later I sought out the individuals whose names had been mentioned. Those who had not passed on to better fishing grounds, I generally found to be sociable, hard-working family men, each with a quick sense of humor. Most were not shy about discussing their frequent brushes with officers of the law, whom they consistently call "the man," nor were they inhibited about sharing their views on ecology and the management of natural resources. What they see as a common-sense approach to living and working with nature is often at odds with positions taken by legislators and the DNR. Here are a few of their stories and comments.

"They never shot at me," the alleged target of the warden's bullets denied that legend, "but they chased me a lot—used to run me all up and down that river. They thought they knew who I was but they never got me. I had a boat would do fifty.

"We did have a lot of nights. I had seventeen after me one time. Yep! But we had little boats here and there and I knew where they were comin' from.

We had CB radios when they first come out. Anytime a boat a-runnin' got within half-a-mile of me, my radio would pick it up—the static, you know, of that outboard. Then I'd whiz off and hide.

"They were tryin' to catch us one night. We knew where they were at, so we thought we'd play with 'em a little. We'd get on the radio and say, 'You go so-and-so place.' By God, there they would come, just like that. Another night they chased me about ten or twelve miles.

"One time it happened to be a real rainy, cold night. We were sittin' up in the Nanticoke Inn drinkin' and playin' cards, and *the man* was out on the river lookin' for us. Later, when we came down to the dock in the pickup, here he comes. It was still rainin' and he come up to the truck and looked in the window. 'Man,' he said, 'if this ain't a fine lookin' group,' and water was runnin' out the ass of his pants.

"A few years ago—after it was all over with—*the man* come over to the boat one day and checked my arsters. He looked at me and says, 'I'd like to ask you somethin'. How'd you know where we were all the time?'

"I said, 'Don't you understand that? My CB radio would pick you up half-a-mile away.'

"He threw his hand down and said, 'I told [a DNR sergeant's name], and he wouldn't believe it.'

"There used to be this truck comin' out of Crisfield, goin' to New York, and we'd meet him in Seaford and load our fish on him. Isaac pulled in there one night with a load of fish in the back—them old big ones, you know. Tails was stickin' up everywhere. And up pulled this car with all these antennas on there. Course Isaac, he didn't know nothin'.

"*The man* asked him—said, 'Captain, what time does that fish truck come through here?'

"'Oh,' Isaac tells him, 'it'll be here 'bout five minutes.'

"Here he's talkin' to *the* federal *man* and don't know it. The truck pulled up there and *the man* nailed 'em all.

"We went to Bridgeville one night—off the back road. We were haulin' oversized rock and we'd changed our loadin' spot. We just got the last box of fish on there and I seen this blue light a-comin. He had it right into 'er. He hit the brake when he come on and slid sideways up to us. It was a state trooper.

"'What are you boys doin'?' he said.

"'We're loadin' fish on this truck. We gen'rally meet right on the highway there, but the traffic's bad, so we thought we'd load up on this back road here.'

"He went and looked in the trucks and seen all these fish in there. 'Well,' he said, 'I want your names,' and he started writin' 'em down—six or seven of us there.

"What happened was: 'bout a week before that they lost a whole bunch of motorcycles—somebody broke in a place and stole 'em— and they loaded 'em on a trailer. He thought that's what we were doin'. We never did hear nothin' from *the man*.

"It's gettin' too many rock out there now. What they do is, they give us a season on 'em, and most of the season they give us don't do us no good 'cause it's not the time to catch 'em. They're not where you want 'em at, and you lose a lot of fish that way. They know. They understand. It's just the money into it—big organizations that's against the watermen. It's these people that...well, the sportsmen, the charter boats—all them with the money."

"I've worked on the water all my life," another weathered old captain told me, "and that's all I know how to do, but it ain't been much to work for the last couple of years, and I'll tell you where a lot of it is. A lot of it is mismanagement of the bay. They got to get their boots on the right feet and change up two or three things to help the bay out. One is to put a limit on the catch. If they put a limit on the crab catch, that'll take a lot of the pots off the bay. Hell, they got 'em ten foot apart out there, and it's just too much. And down to Virginia they catch them sponge crabs [egg-bearing females] up. It shouldn't be allowed."

Tales of avoiding arrest are often told with considerable pride.

"The closest *the man* ever come to catchin' me and not catchin' me on the river: Cecil and I had our boats up in the Northwest Fork. It was like nine o'clock at night and Cecil had a bunch of oversized rock on his boat. Jack comes on the CB and says, 'Mac, I just heard a police boat on my scanner say there's a big white boat in the Fork and they're goin' over there and catch him. *The man* said they were up to somethin' 'cause they pulled in there and shut their lights off.'

"We just had pulled up there and shut our lights off when Jack radioed that. I called over to Cecil: 'They're on the way!'

"About that time I could hear *the man* start up. He was on the other end of the Fork and he wound 'er right up.

"Well, we started out. We were runnin' down the river and Cecil was throwin' his fish overboard left and right. Before they got to us, the police boat started hittin' Cecil's fish—whumpity-whump, whumpity-whump—and *the man* had to slow down. When he finally caught up, we was goin' along just like we didn't even know he was around. He pulled alongside and looked in Cecil's boat. 'I don't know what you boys is up to,' he said, 'but I'm gonna find out.'

"They caught my brother one mornin' with a bunch of rock. Chuckie and myself was still out on the river and I probably had about fifteen hundred pound stashed down in the bow. She was ridin' a little bow heavy anyhow.

"When we come in, my mother run down to the wharf. 'They just got your brother,' she said. 'They were waitin' for him when he come in. If you boys has got any fish on that boat, you get rid of 'em. I'm gettin' tired worryin' about it.'

"Well, we didn't hardly know which way to go. I said to Chuckie: 'I'll tell you what let's do. We'll tie up like usual. Don't make no moves; just act normal.'

"Well, we tied up there at that dock, and just as soon as we threw the rope on the first pilin', here come *the man* in a marine police vehicle, just as hard as they could come down there.

"Chuckie said, 'Back off! Back off! Here they come!'

"I said, 'It ain't no use to back off now; they're here. If I back off now, we'll have a Whaler [DNR boat] on each side of us somewhere down the river.' I could see a sergeant and another one or two there. I said, 'Just tie 'er up and shut 'er off.'

"Here they come, runnin' down on the wharf and lookin' all over the boat. We only had two or three hundred pound of legal fish showin'.

"*The man* says, 'Is that all you fellows caught?'

"I said, 'We haven't seen too much. Come on aboard and have a cup of coffee with us.'

"Well, Chuckie had a cup of coffee in his hand, and the sergeant stepped on that boat and walked right over to the hatch where the big fish was stacked below. Chuckie was drinkin' that coffee and his teeth was a-goin' click! click! click! click! on his coffee cup; I mean they was just a-clickin' away.

"The sergeant says, 'No, I don't believe I want no coffee. You mean to say you boys ain't seen no big rock?'

"I said, 'No, I ain't seen but two or three.'

"He said, 'It's a funny thing; we just got your brother with like a thousand pound.'

"I said, 'Look, just 'cause there's one bad root in the family, it don't mean every root on the tree is bad.'

"Well, he hangs around there a little bit and then he left. I took them fish and up in Delaware I went with 'em. They didn't nobody bother you up in Delaware at that time. We would call this fella and then we'd haul our fish up a creek above the line, and he would come and get 'em. We hauled truckloads in there.

"After a while, when they got after us so tight, we started filletin' them big fish on the boat and puttin' 'em in a plastic bag inside a grass sack. We'd work at nights in small boats. We'd take a high water and go up the creek. I had a cullin' board and we used a putty knife to scale the fish with.

"We run out one night and had maybe six or eight hundred pound of fish in the boat, and I went up what we call Molly Horn Creek. I shut the lights out and we got way up there. There's a fork in the creek and that's about as far as you can go on high water. We got right there to the point of that fork and I shut the motor down. I told Chuckie: 'Go ahead and start scalin' 'em.' Chuckie throwed the cullin' board up there and got ready to scale that first fish. There weren't a light or nothin' on, and a owl says, 'Whooo, whooo.' When he did that, Chuckie like to run right out the boat. I said, 'Chuckie, come on back; it ain't nothin' but a booby owl.'

"There was a marine police out of Delaware one time, and he was as big an outlaw as anybody else. He was a likable character, and I got to know him and carry on with him. We took him out huntin' one time and got to shootin' geese, and he didn't wanna quit.

"He come up to me one day and says, 'Boy, you gonna have a hard time of it now, Captain.'

"I says, 'What's wrong?'

"He says, 'They've got me patrollin' the Nanticoke, and I'm gonna break some of this outlawin' up in there.'

"I was fishin' after that one day and here come a police boat. It come right up beside me, and it was him. He said, 'Well, where's all these big rock?'

"I said, 'Sit here a minute and I'll show you what one looks like.'

"So eventually we caught one and *the man* says, 'Slide him over here and let me look at it.' I slid him over there and *the man* throwed it right in his boat. He said, 'Get me another'n.'

"I wouldn't o' missed that era for nothin', but I don't believe I'd want to go through it again. I quit foolin' with them things after the federal government got in there. It used to cost you $25 and you went out and done it again, but now they don't do it that way."

Marguerite Whilden (left) and Jan Elmy Admire a Terrapin Hatchling

What's Not to Like about a Turtle

"I was horrified!" Elliott-Island artist Jan Elmy said of her trip to mail a package on June 1. "It was awful! I had seen the county mowers come by earlier, and when I drove up to Vienna, there were dead terrapins all over the road. At one point I counted seventeen in less that two miles, and I know there were many more in the grass and flung out in the marsh. I'm sure they killed at least a hundred."

When she caught up with the tractors that were mowing the edge of the causeway between Elliott and Vienna, her first inclination was to block them. "But I was afraid I would go to jail," Elmy said, "and I couldn't afford that." That afternoon she muddled through her tasks, feeling a miserable failure for not having acted.

Hoping to modify the mowing schedule in Dorchester marshes to fit around the peak of terrapin nesting season, Elmy appealed to the county roads superintendent, who promised to speak to his operators and delay cutting, but mowing continued on the marsh causeway two days later.

"I talked to [environmental writer] Tom Horton," Elmy said, "and he put me in touch with Marguerite Whilden."

Born at the Naval Academy and raised in Annapolis, Whilden's background is in habitat engineering. When she first came to the

Eastern Shore marshes twenty-five years ago, Whilden was employed by the Maryland Department of Natural Resources as state coordinator for the National Flood Insurance Program. After fifteen years of advising flood-plain residents, she briefly served as Wetland Manager before assuming her present post with DNR's Conservation and Stewardship Program of the Fisheries Service.

Whether dispensing information or appealing for assistance to industry, watermen, sportsmen, politicians, the general public, or rolling up her sleeves and getting her hands dirty in the field, Whilden's passion for the terrapin shines as brightly as any Chesapeake beacon. Like the smile on the faces of her aquatic wards, her enthusiasm is contagious. "What's not to like about a turtle," she asks.

When invited to attend President Clinton's visit to Assateague Park, she accepted and showed up with several terrapins. Whilden had no difficulty passing the clearance check but her companions flunked. "Well, the turtles might be a security risk," she was told. Unfazed, she took advantage of the opportunity to persuade Congressman Wayne Gilchrest to join her Terrapin Consortium while dignitaries cowered under a sandstorm raised by six presidential helicopters.

On the surface it may seem absurd to attempt a comparison between a six-inch-long turtle and the American bison but, like the buffalo, the diamondback terrapin is a national icon of historic abundance which was nearly lost.

Hailed as a jewel of Chesapeake Bay marshes, the diamondback is among the handsomest of turtles. Highly variable in color, a terrapin's boldly patterned, wedge-shaped carapace ranges from nearly black through shades of brown to milky gray, sometimes showing splashes of yellow, beige or tan. Thirteen large scales called scutes are inscribed by concentric, diamond-shaped rings and give the terrapin its name. The underside or plastron may be orange or yellow to olive, with or without bold, dark markings. The skin is usually pale gray—sometimes white—and is commonly peppered with black flecks and lines that, like human fingerprints, create a design unique to each individual. Docile and prettier than a seashell, the diamondback presents an unassuming face accented by a pair of dreamy eyes and creased by an infectious grin.

Adult male terrapins generally measure six inches in length and weigh half a pound. Females are larger—up to nine inches—and average two pounds. Their webbed feet make them agile swimmers, and sharp claws assist their movement about the marshes. They are a highly aquatic species, seen out of water only when they bask or are nesting.

Of the 270 species of turtles in the world, diamondbacks are the only one which can tolerate both salt and fresh water and whose habitat is restricted to brackish water marshes. They are unique among reptiles in that they possess salt-excluding glands in the corners of their eyes, which develop after their first year of living mostly in fresh water. The species is confined to the United States and ranges from Cape Cod to the Florida Keys and around the Gulf Coast to Texas. Seven subspecies vary in coloration, marking and behavior.

Food preferences among diamondbacks are broad and include live snails, worms, crabs, insects, shellfish, crustaceans and small fishes as well as carrion.

With the first cold temperatures in November, terrapins bury themselves in the mud beneath bay waters, commonly in groups, where they remain through the following March. While their metabolism and body functions are slowed during hibernation to the point where they do not need to breathe, oxygen is absorbed through parts of the turtle's tissue. Because terrapins are occasionally observed in late winter, it is believed that some may simply lie suspended in the water or on the floor of the bay and therefore respond more quickly to the first warm days.

Shortly after emergence from hibernation, terrapins begin to mate. Females may reach sexual maturity in eight years—males earlier. Breeding takes place in May, always in the water and usually at night, and fertilized females can produce eggs up to four years after a single mating.

Most eggs are laid from June to July on sandy borders of coastal salt marshes or in dunes. Multiple clutches are possible, sometimes as close as two weeks apart. Maximum laying activity usually occurs at high tide, ensuring that the clutch will be above the high water level. The female digs a cavity four to eight inches deep and deposits from four to eighteen pinkish-white eggs.

Incubation takes nine to fifteen weeks, and hatchlings the size of a quarter enter the world patterned very much like adults. As with most turtles, temperature influences the individual's sex: High temperatures during incubation produce more female hatchlings, while low readings result in a preponderance of males. If hatched late in the season, the young may remain in the nest for the first winter, emerging in April and May.

It appears that only one to three percent of terrapin eggs hatch, owing largely to predation by foxes, skunks and raccoons, which dig into the nests and consume the eggs and baby terrapins. Survivors emerging from the nest are often eaten by gulls and crows or by herons and predatory fish after entering the water.

The life expectancy of a diamondback is usually estimated at between twenty-five and forty years. Terrapins are known to have survived to the age of fifty, but no one is certain of their maximum potential.

Colonists learned from Native Americans to roast terrapin in live coals. Abundant and easy to catch—a wagon-full could be purchased for as little as a dollar—they became a staple in the diet of many slaves and indentured servants. Contracts limiting the number of terrapin meals that servants could be fed each week have been found. Although Washington and Lafayette are said to have discussed strategy over a meal of Chesapeake terrapin on the eve of the Battle of Yorktown, the turtles were generally considered to be inferior cuisine.

Then, in the late nineteenth and early twentieth centuries, terrapin stew and soup laced with cream and sherry became a delicacy, and the subsequent retail demand and inflated prices resulted in the capture of huge numbers of the turtles, severely depleting their numbers and nearly extirpating them in some areas. Crisfield, Maryland, was the principal supplier to the nation's major cities.

While the fad for terrapin flesh has waned, this docile reptile continues to face a number of threats, especially from habitat destruction, road mortality and drowning in crab traps.

The latter hazard appears to be the most acute. In Maryland, a Patuxent River study indicated that non-commercial crab pots placed by property owners were drowning terrapins at a rate that could have wiped out the river's population in three to five years. The problem exists everywhere that crabs are trapped. A New Jersey survey revealed a loss of 11,000 terrapins a year at one location, and estimates at Charleston, South Carolina, suggested a daily catch by commercial crabbers of 2,500, with a mortality of 10% in pots that were checked every twenty-four hours. If not emptied daily, the kill is nearly 100%. Two-by-five-inch wire excluders on trap entrances prevent turtles from entering without significantly affecting the number or size of crabs captured, but the devices are required only in Maryland and New Jersey at present.

Traditional nesting areas have been severely altered by waterfront development. Even tire tracks from vehicles driven on the sand pose a hazard to hatchlings, which can be trapped in the depressions and die before reaching water.

While incidental kills by motor boats also take a toll, road mortality of nesting females in some areas is higher than their rate of replacement. In a six-year study conducted on part of the Cape May Peninsula, 4,020 road kills were recorded. In another year, 772 terrapins met the same fate.

Terrapin season is now closed in Maryland from May 1 through July 31 to allow for mating and nesting, and terrapins harvested from August to May must be at least six inches long on the plastron. Individuals without a waterman's license are permitted to claim a total of three as pets. By law, eggs may not be disturbed or possessed.

While fisheries problems mount in an increasingly metropolitan state, traditional constituents—sportsmen, charter-boat captains and commercial watermen—are declining in number. Maryland Fisheries Services has initiated the Terrapin Station as an outreach program, aimed primarily at that larger segment of the public that is not directly involved with wildlife. While the project spotlights the terrapin, it is intended to incorporate a full range of fisheries management issues.

The Terrapin Research Consortium was organized by the Terrapin Station to develop sound research, management and educational standards and share information in the interest of the diamondback terrapin. This advisory group is comprised of individuals with expertise in a variety of disciplines and includes Marylanders Whilden, Congressman Wayne Gilchrest, author Tom Horton, veterinarian of exotics Bill Boyd, waterman and biologist Robert Evans, land management expert Kevin Smith and researchers from Georgia, North Carolina, New Jersey, Ohio, Massachusetts and Washington, DC.

One of Whilden's pet projects is the Headstart Program. Terrapin eggs are removed from endangered nests and incubated under controlled conditions. Hatchlings are then assigned to foster parents to raise for a year under the supervision of a mentor and an established protocol, providing the little ones with a better chance of survival in the wild after release.

Elmy and Whilden, who jokingly refer to themselves as the "Thelma and Louise of terrapindom," are well on their way to recouping some of the mowing losses in the Elliott Island marshes. Elmy was successful in incubating 169 of 187 rescued terrapin eggs, and all but the five she is raising herself have been placed in foster homes. "I really miss them," Elmy said. "I hate not knowing what will become of them."

More than fifty years ago, in "Wildlife in American Culture," Aldo Leopold wrote: "In the biological field the sport-value of amateur research is just beginning to be realized." He was speaking about an amateur ornithologist who had made significant contributions through his observations.

"Terrapin work is well suited to this type of outside research," observes Whilden. "Elmy has already validated an hypothesis we have considered. On Elliott, the terrapins ignore what appears to be a very adequate south beach in favor of the north-facing beach, where they have laid clutches on steep cliffs that would normally be ignored. They seem to have learned over time which beach has the best nursery nearby. The north beach provides a source of fresh water, which is absent on the south, and hatchlings need fresh water during the first year when they have not yet developed their salt processing ability."

The diamondback is Maryland's state reptile and also mascot of the University of Maryland at College Park. It all began in 1932 when football coach Dr. H. Curley Byrd recommended adoption of the diamondback, and Maryland teams, previously known as the Old Liners, became the Terrapins.

As a graduation gift from the class of 1933, a terrapin statue was cast from three hundred pounds of bronze by Sculptor Aristide Cianfrani, who used a live Chesapeake diamondback for reference. On May 23, 1933, the mascot was unveiled to the world when the model terrapin—by tugging on a ribbon—pulled a cover from its huge replica. The icon was named Testudo, Latin for the protective headgear worn by Roman soldiers and the source of the scientific classification for turtles—the order testudines.

At first, Testudo sat on a pedestal in front of Ritchie Coliseum, where he became the target of frequent paintings and other deface-ment by rival schools. Then, in 1947, the bronze terrapin fell victim to kidnappers from Johns Hopkins University. When scores of Ma-ryland students rushed to Baltimore and laid siege to the Hopkins campus, two hundred city police were called to control the riot, but the confrontation quickly evolved into a party.

Shortly afterward, Testudo was again snatched and remained missing for two years. Finally discovered on the lawn of a University of Virginia fraternity house, the mascot was retrieved and hidden in a campus carpentry shed at College Park until 1951.

After being filled with seven hundred pounds of concrete, Tes-tudo was attached with steel rods to a new perch in front of Byrd Stadium. Then, with the construction of McKeldin Library in the 1960s, Maryland's most famous terrapin was triumphantly carried to a new pedestal in front of the library and has since cast its un-blinking gaze over McKeldin Mall.

Rubbing Testudo's nose is purported to bring good luck, and legend insists that if a virgin ever graduates from Maryland, Testu-do will sprout wings and fly over the campus.

An Old Pedagogue

After John S. Hill died in 1937, an unpublished manuscript of ten stories about Maryland's Eastern Shore was discovered among his possessions. They are tales of Hill's childhood and a few from his forty-five-year career of teaching and administration in Maryland's public schools.

One of Hill's teachers in Snow Hill had been James R. Townsend, whom Hill eventually replaced. Having acquired an education chiefly by his own effort and outside of a school setting, Townsend was, in many respects, a remarkable person. He was apparently a gentle, lovable, laughable and sometimes eccentric man who looked on the bright side of every difficulty and found humor in it. Though he brooked no lack of respect nor slight to his prerogatives as a teacher from anyone, he was a just man who commanded his students' respect and gratitude by his sympathetic kindness and personal interest in the welfare of each of them. Those who desired and tried to succeed always found a friend and willing helper in Jim Townsend.

While some of Townsend's disciplinary methods would certainly bring him to a confrontation with parents and superiors today—if not with the courts—we can view them with humor in the context of their time. I shall share a few encounters between this old pedagogue and a pupil known as Grissel.

Townsend lived and taught at a time when individual slates were used by pupils to do their calculations for the teacher's inspection. After the work had been passed upon, the slate would be cleaned for the next lesson. Usually this task was accomplished by the simple process of spitting on the slate, rubbing out the work with one's hand and drying the surface with a sleeve.

One day, when Townsend was looking at sums on Grissel's slate, the boy made a remark in what the teacher considered to be a disrespectful manner. Instantly, the slate came down on Grissel's head with sufficient force to break it, leaving the frame dangling about the boy's neck.

"Don't take it off," the teacher admonished Grissel, "till I tell you to do so, unless you wish me to dress you down with my ruler."

Reaching into his pocket and extracting a few coins, Townsend then directed the boy: "Take this fifteen cents and go to Mr. Selby's store and buy a slate as near the size of this one as you can get, but keep that pretty wooden collar around your neck while going and coming and while there. I'll see you going and coming back, and I'll ask Mr. Selby about the time you are there. Be back in twenty minutes and do as I say, unless you want to try the ruler when you return."

Grissel left and returned within twenty minutes, still wearing the slate frame, and he wore the ornament until school was dismissed that day, when, much to his relief, he was permitted to remove it.

Grissel was persistently mischievous—some said bad—and his will seemed to be constantly pitted against that of school authorities. One day the geography class was seated on a long bench in front of the teacher's platform, with Grissel near the middle, directly in front of the teacher's desk. This desk was so large that a boy could get into it, and one sometimes did of his own accord. At other times, Townsend might chuck a pupil into the desk and shut him up as punishment for wrongdoing.

On this occasion, Grissel had a reason for choosing his seat, for he did not know the lesson and thought it possible to keep his book open to the map without being detected. Sitting in his chair, Mr. Townsend could barely see the boy's eyes when he sat upright, but it did not occur to Grissel that the teacher could view his wide-open book *under* the desk. Grissel sat with his elbows planted on the open pages and bent forward so that he might easily scan them.

Townsend took his customary position for comfort—chair tilted back, feet resting on the front edge of the desk and his body nearly horizontal. Grissel sat entirely oblivious to the fact that his little trick was being observed, until the teacher suddenly lunged forward, pushing the heavy desk over on Grissel's bowed shoulders and pinning him down so that the boy could neither rise nor close his book.

With his peculiar grin, Townsend drawled, "Why, Grissel, you simple Jack-a-nape, did you think you could peep in your book and not get caught? But you are caught, you see. And what do you think and how do you feel now?"

Getting more and more uncomfortable under the heavy desk and feeling quite embarrassed because of the hearty laughter of the other students, Grissel blurted, "Let me up, Mr. Townsend, and I won't ever try to cheat again."

"All right, Grissel," the teacher answered. "Whatever else may be said of you, I believe no one can truthfully say that you ever lie, even if you did try to cheat just then. You have promised not to cheat again and I trust you."

The other boys were then directed to lift the desk off Grissel's shoulders.

Townsend prided himself on his success with teaching boys to "speak pieces" on Friday afternoons and special occasions. He seemed to be in full accord, at least in some respects, with that matchless orator of all ages, Demosthenes, who, when asked to give the first essential principle for public speaking, promptly answered, "Action." When asked for the second, he again called, "Action," and when queried for the third, he shouted, "Action!" Jim Townsend also believed in action in public speaking. He reveled in tragic selections and was untiring in showing appropriate gestures for each line and almost each word.

"In my imagination," Hill reported, "I can see Mr. Townsend now as he stood on his platform one day, showing a boy the correct tones, inflections and gestures to be used in speaking that old favorite 'Casabianca' by Mrs. Hemans, which is better known, perhaps, by its first line: 'The boy stood on the burning deck.'"

Just as Townsend was about to begin rehearsal of this declamation, Grissel came to his desk, ostensibly to request assistance regarding a problem in arithmetic but really in search of fun and mischief.

When Grissel was directed to return to his desk and come for help later, he turned as if to go but stopped on the platform behind the teacher to await his opportunity.

Believing that Townsend would not think of him again nor notice his presence upon the platform, Grissel stood behind the teacher, following and imitating his gestures throughout the rehearsal, though he greatly exaggerated, grossly caricatured and comically mimicked every action and pose. The boy worked his lips and mouth as if speaking and gave such contortions to his face and body as to make a veritable clown of himself. He threw his arms wildly around and jumped and pranced about. Grissel's actions so much exceeded those of the teacher that the attention of every pupil was soon centered upon the boy. Although the class endeavored not to give the showman away by laughing outright, it was constantly on the verge of explosion.

In spite of the fact that Townsend proceeded as though unconscious of any unusual activity, the pupils' half-suppressed merriment was evident to him. He became more and more violent in his gestures, as if he intended, indeed, to make action the rule of his speaking. The teacher's hands and arms flew wildly, now this way, now that, while Grissel's hands were even more animated. Thus the two went on, back and forth, up and down, until they reached that tragic line: "The boy, oh, where was he?"

At that point, Townsend stepped quickly to his rear and made a tremendous backward sweep with his arms. His left arm struck Grissel squarely across the face and knocked the boy sprawling on the floor. The students could restrain themselves no longer and fifty boys and girls roared with laughter at Grissel's downfall. For a moment or two the teacher ceased speaking and stood as if in the greatest surprise, gazing upon Grissel, who was trying to collect his scattered wits sufficiently to rise and make off to his desk.

"Why, Grissel," the teacher at last exclaimed, apparently in astonishment, "did I do that? Where were you, Grissel, and what were you doing there that I should blunder against you? Please pardon my clumsy gesture and tell us how it all happened."

But Grissel was limping back to his desk, crestfallen.

A few days later, a boy called Peck, who, like Grissel, was almost constantly getting into trouble, came to school early one morning with a small pasteboard box in his pocket in which he had managed to imprison four or five bumblebees.

Only Grissel and one or two of his pals were at school when Peck arrived and slyly showed Grissel his treasures. At once Grissel had an idea. Taking Peck aside, Grissel whispered something to him, which pleased Peck so much that he immediately handed over the box of bees. Unseen by the others, Grissel transferred one bee to a matchbox without its cover, but safely wrapped in a sheet of paper on which he had written something. This box he slipped into his pocket. The other, which still contained three or four bees, Grissel placed inside the teacher's desk, first having set the cover of the box askew to allow the bees to crawl out. Then he shut the desk lid and awaited developments.

As soon as school was called in, Grissel passed the little box in his pocket to Peck, who unwrapped it and found the word "Stung" written on the paper. As Grissel had expected, the angry bumblebee in the box instantly proceeded to emphasize the message on the paper. With a loud yell, Peck sprang up, trying to fight off the angry bee, and bolted for the door.

Meanwhile, Grissel had sauntered innocently up to the teacher's side to be as far as possible from the danger zone of that bee, pretending that he wanted the loan of a slate pencil. Mr. Townsend kept a number of pencils in his desk for such purposes, and all he had to do was lift the lid a little and run his hand in to take one out. By doing that, he was expected to come in contact with the bees and the fun would begin. To Grissel's surprise and consternation, however, the teacher seized him, lifted the desk lid and dropped the boy in. Mr. Townsend then sat down and propped his feet on the desk to keep the lid closed and the boy contained.

Once in the desk, Grissel thought it best to keep quiet. He hoped the bees might stay in their box or leave the desk through a crack that had been left open for ventilation, but he soon realized the vanity of his expectation. As he reached out to ease his cramped position, his hand came in contact with a bee, which stung him instantly.

"Let me out," Grissel yelled, and while struggling to raise the desk lid, he was stung two or three more times, at each stab e-mitting a nerve-racking scream. Finally, he could stand it no long-er and sprang up like a Jack-in-the-box, upsetting the teacher's chair and rolling him on the floor. Grissel ran for the door, fighting off the enraged bees and causing a pell-mell rush by the other child-ren to escape.

After the bees were disposed of and calm had returned, the work of the day went on. Each of Grissel's hands was the size of two, and his face looked as if he had mumps all over it. Peck was nursing a sore and very swollen hand but, fortunately, no one else was in-jured. It seemed an irony that only the perpetrators of the mischief should have felt the wrath of the bees. "Just retribution," Townsend called it, and since the boys had been so thoroughly stung and the laugh upon them was so merciless, he declared them sufficiently punished and let the matter go at that.

During the time James Townsend taught, he was never rated higher than "second grade," this appraisal being based upon the number of subjects on which he satisfactorily passed an examina-tion given by the county school examiner, and his salary never ex-ceeded $350 for a school year of nine months.

Townsend was a victim of the "white plague" or tuberculosis, which was once so prevalent. Though he knew the disease was gradually killing him, he remained serene and cheerful. Even when wasted and bound to his bed, the old schoolmaster continued to entertain those around him with whimsical chatter.

The English essayist and poet Charles Lamb is said to have died spitting blood and puns, and apparently the same can be said of James Townsend, an old pedagogue from long ago.

John S. Hill's manuscript has been edited by Hal Roth and published in Stories of the Eastern Shore, Nanticoke Books, 2001.

On the Subject of Witches

Several years ago I conducted a series of conversations with a small group of elderly African Americans. After tossing out a leading question, I would turn on a tape recorder and sit back and listen as they talked among themselves about life when they were "coming up." The following exchange on the subject of witches and witchcraft has been edited from several of our gatherings. Altogether, a dozen women and two men participated, but each meeting contained a different mixture. Some of those wonderful folks have since passed on, one of them at the age of 103.

"It was a lot of witches one time. You always heard about somebody put a spell on somebody, but you don't hear much nowadays. Seem like all the witches drop off now. Don't know where it all gone to."

"Yep, a lot of people used to put spells on other people. It's nothin' but the devil in 'em. They read up on things like [that] and tries 'em."

"Yeah, that's what it is. Momma told me about her sister, Aunt Julie. Some woman took and fixed her so she couldn't even walk. The woman went to a fortuneteller and she put a spell on Julie. It been a long time ago, when the steamboat used to travel, and you know it's been a long time since the steamboat traveled.

"Well, she did it on account of a man. This woman wanted the same man that Aunt Julie wanted, and she put a spell on her so she couldn't get him. And I'll tell you one thing: I believe women will do that. A lot of women, they want the man and don't care what it costed. They'll try to get you any way they can.

"Aunt Julie got him after while, but she wouldn't [have] got him if Uncle Exter hadn't come down from Balt'mer. He was Momma's uncle. He lived in Balt'mer, and he seen people like that in the city. He said to Momma's mother: 'You better carry that gal somewhere. Do you know, if you don't carry that gal pretty soon, she gonna die. She can't walk. She gonna crawl up there and couldn't walk, and she gonna die, just on account of a man.'

"My grandmother said, 'I believe in the Lord. The Lord didn't intend for her to be like that. I don't know who coulda done it, but that was some of the devil's work.'

"My mother said to Uncle Exter: 'Why did that woman do it? Why they do stuff like that? In my day they didn't do it.'

"I thought to myself when Mom told him: 'She did it on account of Uncle Eddie.' And her name was Julie, just like Aunt Julie.

"My mother supposed to be religion and everything; she didn't believe nobody could do it like that. Mother said, 'Ain't this somethin'; I never believe people could do you a thing like that. Some of 'em will kill you over a man, I guess.'

"Sometimes when people got all kinds of ways, they let 'em die when they could of went someplace and got rid of whatever they had. Some people went to fortunetellers and some didn't. When Mom come to find out, she carried Aunt Julie to a woman named Emma J. Kenny and Minnie J. Kenny. Minnie was the mother and Emma was the girl. They were both fortunetellers.

"And don't you know, that woman took her hands and rubbed Julie and said, 'I wouldn't have what you had done to you over a man.' Mom said she took her hands and rubbed all down my aunt, and after that woman went down her leg, she got up and walked; Julie got up and started walkin'. Mom said, 'That quick and you walkin'?'

"The fortuneteller woman said, 'Yeah, but if you hadn't brought her, two, three days from now she'd been dead.'

"And Mom said she couldn't believe [it]. She said that Aunt Julie come back there a-walkin', and after she got that spell off'n her, Uncle Exter went to Balt'mer with her on that steamboat.

"And don't you know, my aunt married Uncle Eddie after all. She lived and had twelve head of children, and all of 'em lived to get grown. Now it's only one left and he beats on his wife. He beats on her and she just as nice to him as she can be. He don't even want her to talk on the phone.

"But people had a lot of meanness then, just like now. I don't mean no harm, but a lot of people would rather start fussin' with you, and you didn't have nothin' to do with whatever it is. And don't you know, I've heard the old folks say it more than one time; they got ten thousand way to cheat one soul, and I believe it. They'll do anything [if] they want [to] argue with you. And if you don't argue with 'em, they still try to get you. You be surprised how people will hurt their own people and everybody else for no reason at all.

"It was a few fortunetellers then, but since then it's been a whole lot of 'em. Sometimes people give them two, three thousands of dollars a year to go to 'em. My cousin got bad off one time so she said, 'I think I'm goin' [to] take and go there.' And every year she had to work hard to get that money."

"The fortunetellers would tell you what's gonna happen to you or what somebody done to you or somethin' like that. They would said they knew if somebody put a spell on you, but I never believed in nothin' like that."

"A girl one time pulled a spell on my sister. When the spell happened on her, she go, 'Ahhhh,' and can't help it. She eat a piece of candy and that would stop it. They was drinkin', you know, like a sociable drink—like that—and that girl slip somethin' in her cup. I carried her to the hospital for it. I ask her what was the matter and she said, 'Oh, I'm just a-gappin'. Ahhhh,' like that. It was a spell the girl put on her. It was devilish, that's all. The devil was into her. She had a demon in her. But she gets a-gappin' like that and you give her a piece of candy, that cleans it up until the next time it come 'round again."

"A woman told me she went to the fortuneteller for luck, and

87

the fortuneteller give her a little piece of pork bone, you know, them little round pork bones. She give her that for luck and the woman said she didn't have no luck. The fortuneteller just eats the pork off the bone and give her the bone, just to take her money."

"That's how the fortunetellers make their money. Some people wind up comin' and see 'em reg'lar and payin' thousand dollars, and some people live and died and never gone to 'em at all."

"It didn't cost a lot of money to go to some fortunetellers. They'd take chickens or anything as payments. They just wanted to live too. But they got so they want to make money now."

"Whatever the fortunetellers told, people would believe it. It used to be [that] old women would tell fortunes. They believed the old women could tell your fortune."

"And some people broke up families like that. They say somebody gonna run your wife or gonna run your husband and they believed it. They'd tell your fortune in your hand, like this mark and that mark in your hand."

"They thought these old women with long dresses and their heads wrapped up—thought they was witches and they could put a spell on somebody. It would make 'em crazy and make 'em act silly. They'd go to fortunetellers to get it off."

"Well, I never did believe into all that. They thought somebody had put a spell on 'em, but it was just old age workin' on 'em. Old age was makin' 'em ill and they thought somebody was puttin' somethin' on 'em. It was just nature."

"We'd be sittin' 'round the fire and people would talk about they saw a witch and what they did."

"Did you ever hear of a high man?"

"I heard one time he tricks a woman to run rabbits through the woods like a dog, 'arw, arw, arw, arw,' just run through the woods tryin' to catch a rabbit, but that's all I heard about anything like that. I never hear talk of she catchin' one. A rabbit can go so fast. That would be a spell."

"You put a broomstick 'cross the door to keep the witches from ridin'. My mother used to have trouble with witches. She'd get all nervous and like she was havin' a dream or somethin'. And when she would do that, sometime I would shake her."

"It's like they say, witches will ride you, yes, indeed. I hear a lot of people say you have to put a broom across the door. And another thing you can do is take your Bible and put it to the 121st Psalm and put it underneath your pillow. I know I don't want no witches ridin' me. When witches ride you, you can't say nothin' and you can't move; you just goin' in a dream. You don't know what you doin'. You can't open your mouth."

"I used to have a witch to ride me all the time. I couldn't get up. Come hop right on top of you. You just layin' down there and she ridin' you so bad you sayin' everything: 'Ehhh, uhhh, yehhh, uhhh.'"

"I heared that if you put a broom across the door, it keep the witches out, but it's just somethin' somebody made up; wasn't no such thing as witches. It's like Santa Claus. I thought it was so 'cause I didn't think Mom and Pop would tell nothin' wrong."

"No, it's really true about the witches because I had to take my mother and I know, but the broom most will solve the problem. I know a man right across from me; he had to keep his broom to the door every night. If he didn't, the witches would ride him."

"Did they do somethin' else beside ride you?"

"I don't know. I didn't give 'em no chance."

"If your horse had knots in his tail, that means a witch was ridin' it."

"I heard that a witch could turn people into horses."

"Witches don't go for a sifter—thing you sift the flour with. They don't like a sifter no way."

"The old folks all used to say there were witches. My father's aunt—they would say she was a witch. She come, and you would stick pins in the bottom of the chair. She set down on that chair and she couldn't move until you get the pins out from underneath of her. Somebody shot her in the mouth after that."

"I know a man married this woman one time. She was a real nice lookin' woman. He married her and he didn't know she was a graveyard digger. He notice she don't eat nothin'. He thought, 'What's the matter with her?' One time it was late at night and he look for her, and she gone. She gone to the graveyard twelve o'-clock at night [to] get her some dead people. So he went out there and catch her. She come back in and pull her legs off. They was artificial. He marry a artificial woman! She pull everything off. She was a witch and a graveyard digger, and she ate dead folks. He left her after that."

"My father and his friends were skatin' one day—they liked to skate all night—and he said they seen a witch, bless God, and she was singin' 'Who's sorry now.' And boy, they fell off their skates and got away from there. They was scared."

"For witches, my father said you take flax seed and turn it over and you can catch 'em. Turn the flaxseed over and she got to count every one of those flaxseed before she can leave. When the mornin' come, you can find out who it is. She'll be there pickin' them flaxseed up.

"This woman's husband would go away and be goin' out late, and she couldn't find him. One night she had this flaxseed and turned it over, and she said the next mornin' she seen this cat, and it was all around her feet. So she took a dustpan and took those flaxseed up and threw 'em in the trash can. She start hittin' on that cat with the dustpan and shook him up, and he come back as his own self—real. The cat was her husband. Her husband was there, pickin' up the flaxseed, and he turned into a cat. He was bewitched. She says, 'Uh huh, you devil you, I caught you tom-cattin' around.' She says, 'I know just who you is, you witch you!'"

"I wouldn't want him no more."

"Me neither!"

"They say the witch could come through the keyhole or somethin', but that's not possible, I don't think."

"I don't know; they could do most anything. A witch pulled this man's shoes off one time; he told me that."

"They said some people was witches. You'd see a person that dress funny and act funny, they'd say they was witches and they would cast spells. That's what they said they would do. Yes, indeed, they said they could do that. And they say cats are witches friends—a black one. If a black cat crosses 'em, they'll turn around.

Yes, indeed they will. Some of 'em [are] still superstitious about that."

"I say they ain't no witches; it's just in somebody's head."

"Well, you better think on it. One jumps in your bed, you know 'bout it then."

Creating a Legend

The *Random House Dictionary of the English Language* defines legend as a "nonhistorical or unverifiable story handed down by tradition from earlier times and popularly accepted as historical." Legends and fables and myths fill our literature and folklore.

Historical figures sometimes gain legendary status as their exploits are retold and expanded from generation to generation. We can document the fact that a real-life frontiersman by the name of Davy Crockett died while defending the Alamo, but did he also kill him a bear when he was only three?

Other legends spring purely from the imagination of storytellers or are based on obscure or unidentifiable characters. Paul Bunyan, the giant, ax-wielding woodsman, and his companion Babe, the blue ox, are products of the rugged humor of northern lumberjacks, who created their own entertainment around glowing wood stoves in their pine-log shanties on cold winter evenings. Local embellishments were added as the tales spread until the colossal figures of Paul and Babe became idols to nearly every child in the nation.

Not all legends gain the status of Davy Crockett and Paul Bunyan. Many have their roots in old country stores that once served as rural centers for community news and entertainment and are circulated among a mere handful of people. Innumerable, unrecorded yarns have been created on those wonderful stages by and about just plain folks, whose deeds, fact or fancy, have stirred someone's imagination.

Among the legions of local folk heroes are a few individuals who began their ascent to fame through tongue-in-cheek tales they told about themselves. I encountered one such individual in the community of Galestown, Maryland, tucked away near the Nanticoke River in Dorchester County.

"He was a carpenter and a builder of boats by trade," I was told early one morning over a cup of coffee in Wheedleton's Seafood Market and Country Store. "John Stevens could build most anything that come along. He could get a piece of lumber right between his feet and take an adz and work it out, and you'd think a plane run over it; it was that smooth." Among the products of his craft, my informant claimed, were the sleek, now almost legendary shad barges that once graced nearly every wharf along the Nanticoke River.

Years ago, when it was plentiful in swamps along Delmarva rivers, white cedar was the wood of choice for many boat builders. "If John was up a creek and seen a tree he wanted," I was told, "what he did was, he had this winch on his shad barge—a great big, hand-cranked winch. He'd cut that tree and winch that log out of the cripples and tow it out of the creek." Stevens had, of course, no permission to cut the timber, his fans will add with a grin.

Ask anyone in Galestown about John Stevens and the response will likely go something like this: "John was a good old thing. He'd do anything in the world for you if he liked you." I have also been told that if he didn't like you: "Just forget about it."

While he is touted as a master carpenter and boat builder in his old hometown, whiskey, they will tell you, was his avocation.

Not far above Gales Creek the Nanticoke River curves through an S-bend into Delaware. Inside the first loop, on the state line between Sussex and Wicomico Counties, what appears as a point of land is really an island of pinewoods and cripples, detached from the mainland by Cod Creek and Devil's Gut. Some refer to this piece of no-man's land as Patty Cannon's Island. In the first quarter of the nineteenth century, legend claims, the Cannon-Johnson gang kidnapped free blacks and chained them to trees there to await shipment south into slavery.

Tradition is strong in Galestown that John Stevens maintained stills on Patty Cannon's Island. Tom Marine once visited the cripples with John. "He carried us over there to show us the rings and chains on the trees," Tom said. "John kept stills over there during Prohibition. He told us the old barrel staves were rotten and gone, but the iron rims were still there, and he walked right to 'em."

Stevens is said to have told ghost stories about the island to discourage people from going there. "And when I was young," Marine told me, "John used to say that Patty Cannon would sometimes cut the slaves' heads off, and she'd save the blood and sell it to people that made something out of it. That's what John said," Marine nodded for emphasis, "and that's all I got to go by."

"They got after him one time for makin' whiskey on the island," another acquaintance offered, "so he went up to Baltimore. He stayed a couple week, come back and went right on makin' it again. He made whiskey right on up till he died."

"During Prohibition," Eddie Wheedleton repeated a story that he claims Stevens often told, "John worked for a basket factory, and he was takin' gum logs by barge to New York. At that time they kept cats on the tugboats to keep the rats and mice down, so they had this old tomcat that stayed on board.

"Anyway, they pulled the barge in there to New York Harbor, and John had a bunch of liquor on board. He had a market pretty well set up and knew who to go to and who not to. John started off the boat, and he put that old cat in a bag and shook him up right good. The guard stopped him and asked what he had to declare. John said, 'It's just a cat.'

"The guard said, 'I don't believe you,' and he made John open up the bag. When he opened it, the cat run right up the guard's shoulder, over his head and back down on the tug. It scratched the guard right good.

"John went back on the tug and put his liquor in the bag. Then he come up and asked the guard if he wanted to see his tomcat

94

again. The guard told him: 'No, I don't believe I will.'

"John used to pay the boys a little money to pick up pint and half-pint whiskey bottles on the road. He'd wash 'em out and put whiskey into 'em, and he'd take them bottles to New York."

I was told that Stevens had two or three accomplices over the years that worked the stills with him and helped distribute his whiskey and applejack. "He had one fellow with a great big coat with pockets, and he'd go all around with liquor into it. If the cops grabbed him, he could run right out of his coat, just like a skunk runnin' out of his hide. They'd get after the old man and grab for his coat collar, and he was gone."

It is claimed that in the early 1940s John contributed to the war effort by guarding German prisoners at Slaughter's Neck. The story goes that "John would shoot between their feet to make 'em dance and all that kind of mess."

"When he was first assigned to the prison camp, they had a bunch of 'em got sick, and they couldn't tell what they got sick with. The only thing they could get out of any of 'em was 'da biggety bird, da biggety bird.' Come to find out, they killed a buzzard and eat 'im."

John lived between the Galestown Cemetery and the river in an old, wood-frame house that I was told he kept primed with burnt oil. "It was waterproof," my informant chuckled. "Thompson Water Seal ain't got nothin' on burnt oil."

"A fellow come up on his house one time and had to go. 'Where's your bathroom at?' he asked John.

"'Right out there in that field,' Stevens answered.

"Fellow said, 'What do you mean?'

"John said, 'It's like the cat: You go out there and dig a little hole, do your thing and scratch it over.'"

"Cancer killed him," the coffee crowd told me. "He worked in a saw mill and had a tooth off a saw strike him in the face. It never would heal."

After leaving the store, I stopped at the cemetery where Stevens lies at rest, only a short distance from where he once lived. Secured by a red and gold ribbon and topped by red flowers, an attractive spray of evergreens adorned the marble gravestone. To John's side of the marker the casting of a floppy-eared dog looked up at me with wide, questioning eyes, while the silhouette of a black cat stood guard next to his wife Alice's epitaph.

Stevens' only child, Anna, married John Edward Goslee. "He always had a mess of coon dogs around," Goslee told me. "That's why we put the dog there, and Alice liked her cat."

Stevens often spun tales about witchcraft and how he would ride to the moon with an old witch. "That old witch weren't all that bad lookin' one time," he would tell people, "but I'm so ugly that it rubbed right off on her, and now she looks like me."

Stevens lost his teeth at an early age and had the remarkable ability of bringing his chin up—without the use of his hands—to where it would touch his nose. "There, now, don't you see the resemblance?" he would say.

Stevens told these stories without ever cracking a smile and responded angrily if challenged: "Don't you call me no liar!"

"He'd torment Alice right square to death," Goslee said. "When Alice was away one day, John crossed two sticks and laid them under the doormat. When she come back, he told her: 'Don't go over that step. The old witch has been here and give me orders not to move them sticks till midnight.'"

When Alice asked how she was to enter the house, Stevens advised: "The only thing I know is you have to go around the back and crawl in a window."

"After that," Goslee claims, "Alice never come home without she didn't lay that mat up and look."

Stevens was born near East New Market, the son of a self-taught veterinarian and part-time farmer. He never attended school, which was true of many boys from his generation.

In his early years he worked on sailing vessels. "He grew up on one of them," Goslee said. "He'd been to the West Indies and everywhere. And then they had the barges that hauled gum logs out of Dismal Swamp, North Carolina. He was the cook on one of them for a long time."

Stevens was also an auto mechanic. "He'd work for somebody," said Goslee, "and he'd always get in a fight. Patty Cannon would have been glad to have him. He could take on a dozen of the best, strongest men there was, and in five minutes every one would be on the ground. Man, if he ever hit you with his left fist, you were done. In his younger days, he and his brother would rather fight than eat."

"Did John Stevens build shad barges?" I asked his son-in-law, who has crafted a hundred of those unique watercraft and nearly a hundred additional vessels of various other designs.

"He never built a boat in his life," Goslee replied. "During World War II my father hired him. John was driving wells—pitcher-head pumps—and my father got him to go down to his mill at Quantico to drive a pump. John liked the crew, so Dad says, 'If you want a job, I'll give you a job,' and he put him in the woods cutting timber.

"John was pretty good at sharpening saws, and he could cut a tree down and make an ax handle by chopping it out with another ax. Dad had two mills and he kept John busy doing that stuff.

"Later on, Dad moved the mill out of the woods and come up here in Sharptown. John stayed until dad died, and after that he worked with my brother on the farm."

I asked if Stevens had been cut in the face by a saw blade and died from cancer caused by the injury.

"That's true and not true," Goslee replied. "He was running a double edger at the mill one time and a saw tooth—they're insert teeth—come spinning out and got him right center in the lower lip. It left a quarter-inch kerf, and it was just hanging there. We wanted to run him up the street to Doctor Kuhlman, but no, he wasn't going to no doctor. He didn't do a thing in the world but take his pocketknife out and cut the end off, and there was a great big gap in his lip after that.

"But it's not true about the cancer. He held a blamed cigarette on his lip in one place all the time. Back thirty years ago, I expect, he had a skin cancer taken off, and he never had no trouble for years. Then it come back in the same place, and that time it just eat the side of his face, his gums and jawbone and all. We had him up to Hopkins but there was nothing they could do."

"What about the other tales? Did he guard German prisoners at Slaughter's Neck?"

"Oh, now, John was a character," Goslee chuckled. "He could tell some of the greatest mess you ever heard. He'd be telling it and he'd wink at me.

"John worked with the German prisoners in my father's mill. My father used to go down to Westover every morning and bring them to Quantico. It was hard to get help those years. I've heard my father say it was a nice-working bunch of men, and just as friendly. They even wrote to him after they got back. But there was one, you couldn't tell him nothing. He was off bearing. You'd rip the board off'n the log and have an off bearer to carry it out and put it on a pile. He'd always swing the end around. So one morning he started that, and the sawyer hollered at him to be careful. The next time he grabbed a board like that, the lumber caught the saw and yanked him into it—struck him right in the head and split him open. One part went over the sawyer's head and the other...well, it was just a gory mess. John was working there when that happened."

"Did John ever make any whiskey?" I asked.

"He'd make a little for hisself, right there in his shed, but he never made any on Patty Cannon's Island. A friend of his did make it over there, and John would haul it across the river for him because this fellow didn't have a boat. John used to go over in the middle of the night—paddle right out from Galestown. He'd go get the whiskey and set it on the Galestown side of the river, and the man would go pick it up."

"Daddy was just plain old living—no luxuries," Anna Goslee fondly recalled her father. "He kept a small still in the garage and I can remember him drinking a little bit from the end of the coil, but I really doubt that he sold any. It makes a funny story, though, and he might have told it.

"When Daddy was real young and went to work on the boat," Anna said, "his mother sent him a cake. When it got there, it was full of ants, so he waited until it was dark that night to eat it."

I had been told in Galestown that "John was a good old thing," and in Sharptown, where he once worked at the pulpwood yard and sawmill, that fact was verified.

"When people were coming in for their checks one Friday, Avery Owens said to this man: 'You know, it's cold; you should have your jacket on.'

"The man said, 'I don't have one.'

"John took his off and gave it to the man, and he said, 'Here, you take this. I've got another one at home.'"

But if John Stevens is remembered along the Nanticoke River a hundred years from now, I suspect it will be for the legend he created rather than for the legend he was. And by then you can expect his tales to have been even more expertly embellished.

*Lyle Gootee shows the ring and chain to Linda and Donald Allen
in Days Gone By Museum*

Patty Cannon's Island

"**N**ow, I never been by this place before," Jimmy Phoebus muttered, "but by smoke! yon house looks to me like Betty Twiford's Wharf, an' to save my life, I can't help thinkin' yon white spots down this side of the river air Sharptown. If that's the case, which state am I in?"

"He rose to his feet, bailed the scow, which was nearly full of water, and began to paddle along the shore. The sound of someone singing came from the woods nearby. Listening, Phoebus concluded that it was further along the water and he paddled softly forward till he came to a small cove, which led into the swamp. Nowhere did its shores offer a dry landing, yet there were recent footprints deeply trodden in the bog and disclosed up the slope into the woods. The mysterious chanting seemed to come from their direction.

"The trees increased in size as he went on and entered a noble grove of pines, through whose roar, like an organ accompanied by a human voice, the singing was heard nearer and nearer. Following the tracks of previous feet, which had almost made a path, Phoebus came to a space where an axe had laid the smaller bushes low around a large loblolly pine. There, fastened by a chain, which only allowed her to go around the tree and tread a nearly bare place in the pine droppings or shats, a black woman sat, singing in a long, weary, throatsore wail.

"As Phoebus came in sight, she glanced up, looked at him in blank curiosity, as if she did not know what kind of animal he was, then continued her song wearily, as if she had been singing it for days and her mind was out of her control. As she moved her feet from time to time, the chain rattled upon her ankles.

"The chain, strong and rusty, had been very recently welded to her feet by a blacksmith. The fresh rivet attested that, and there were also pieces of charcoal in the pine strewings, as if fire had been brought there for smith's uses. Jimmy Phoebus took hold of the chain and examined it link by link till it depended from a powerful staple driven to the heart of the pine tree. Though rusty, it was perfect in every part, and the condition of the staple showed that it was permanently retained in its position, as if to secure various and successive persons. The staple itself had been driven above the reach of the hands, as by a man standing on some platform or on another's shoulders."

With those words from his 1884 novel, *The Entailed Hat*, George Alfred Townsend introduced the world to an isolated point of swampy terrain on the Nanticoke River that straddles the border between Maryland and Delaware. The setting for his narrative is the first quarter of the nineteenth century, and the female character in chains is a freeborn black woman, who is being detained until such time as she can be shipped south and sold into slavery. She has been kidnapped by cohorts of Patty Cannon, Delmarva's most notorious lady of crime, who died in the Georgetown, Delaware, prison in 1829 while awaiting trial for murder.

The Entailed Hat is a remarkable tapestry, woven from elements of both fact and fiction, and which cleverly intermingles historical personalities with characters forged by Townsend's fertile imagination. Although an extensive search of contemporary documents and writings has been conducted, there appears to be no other nineteenth-century mention of the activities he associates with this still secluded and inhospitable tract that has come to be known as Patty Cannon's Island. Where, then, is the tale properly to be placed: in our history books or in the vast athenaeum of fiction?

As far as I can determine, nearly eighty years passed between publication of *The Entailed Hat* and the first serious attempt to verify Townsend's story. In the early 1960s, writer Ted Giles employed riverman and country storeowner Elijah Wheedleton of Galestown to transport him in a sleek Nanticoke shad barge to the forbidding piece of real estate that Townsend had described.

In his book, *Patty Cannon—Woman of Mystery*, Giles later wrote: "The Story has come down from family to family for more than a hundred years that on these islands Patty Cannon and her gang chained their captives. Great trees, they assert, contained iron rings attached to staples driven into the trees, and held prisoners secure until time for shipment. The trees and rings were there seventy-five years ago; fathers and grandfathers saw them."

But Giles did not find any rings or chains. "We searched the island," he reported, "both on land and from the water. No tree is in sight that could have been a hundred and thirty years of age."

Others claim that the trees survived well into the twentieth century. The late Tom Marine, speaking of the property just below the state line on the Northwest side of the Nanticoke—the same site that Townsend referred to as Betty Twiford's Wharf—once told me: "There was great big trees on the farm, and there was big rings on a wedge drove in there, and they said that's where Patty Cannon used to tie the slaves."

And referring to the island across the river that was searched by Wheedleton and Giles, Marine added: "John Stevens took us to Patty Cannon's Island years back, and there were chains in them trees. I saw the trees, yes sir! They were a big ring with an iron wedge, you might say, and they drove that into a tree. There weren't no chains on the trees on the farm, but if you went across to the island, there were chains hangin' down. Of course they were all rusted."

Those unfamiliar with Nanticoke River topography and tradition will be confused if they come looking for islands. They will find no tracts of land visably surrounded by water. An "island" on the Nanticoke is any dry sector within the swampy cripples that border much of the waterway and is usually distinguishable as a pine grove. Loblollies will not mature where the tide regularly floods.

The name "Patty Cannon's Island" does not appear on any map that I have ever seen. Many who use that term in conversation are alluding to a patch of woodland along the southeastern shore of the Nanticoke that is more commonly known as Tick Island. But to complicate matters further, area residents are not always referring to the same piece of real estate when they talk about Tick Island. For some Galestown residents, Tick Island is the area above Sharptown where the Nanticoke begins a broad S-curve and which is bisected by the Maryland-Delaware boundary line; while a reference to Tick in Sharptown will almost always direct you to the most distinct grove of pines midway between Sharptown and the river bend. Approximately half a mile separates the two points.

Sharptown native John Goslee also claims to have seen hardware and chain imbedded in large pines on the island mentioned by Marine and searched by Giles—the one on the state line. "They were immense in size," Goslee told me, referring to the trees, "and they were rooted right at the edge of the hill. They were five or six foot across the stump. I can see them bolts in my eyes right now; they're so plain. I can't remember seeing anything up high, but down where they shackled their legs to. That was around 1947."

Goslee described the location in these words: "You go up the river past Tick Island and the Delaware line and you come to Cod Creek. Go up Cod Creek, and just in the edge of the cripples, like, you'll see a blind ditch on your right going up. You don't go in there no piece before you make a turn to your right, and when you get to the end of it, you'll come right up on the high ground of Patty Cannon's Island. It's a big hill, a sand hill.

"Patty Cannon and her help dug that ditch themselves. John Stevens always said that was the only way they got in there. The only other way is to go considerable further up the creek till you come to Devil's Gut, but you'd have so far to go in there that it was too much trouble. It was simple just what she did.

"I've heard John speak of Zert Island many a time—as well as my grandfather—and I'd be willing to bet it's the same thing as Patty Cannon's Island from hearing him talk. It probably had that name before Patty Cannon.

"I cannot believe those trees are down. They were so big, but they were short—a lot of branches on 'em. I cannot believe anything different but what they are standing. But as big as they were, if they did blow down, there ought to be some signs there of 'em. I'd love to take one of them bolts out and give it to you. Now that'd be worth a twenty-dollar gold piece, wouldn't it? I don't know why in the world —course you don't see far enough ahead—that I didn't cut every one of 'em out. But they were on Patty Cannon's Island or Zert Island—either one you want to call it—and it weren't Tick Island."

Two nagging questions prevent me from confidently declaring that the testimony offered by Marine and Goslee conclusively proves the existence of Patty Cannon's Island and pinpoints its location. Could a loblolly pine that was mature around 1820 survive for another hundred and thirty years in such an environment? And would a staple and ring in a growing tree still be visible to the eye after thirteen decades? Although its rate of growth slows once a tree has reached fifty or so years, and conditions in the cripples tend to retard that rate even more, it doesn't seem possible for a ring to remain exposed after such a length of time. Steel spikes that protruded six inches from a large loblolly pine in 1974 on my own Dorchester County property have all but disappeared beneath new growth in the ensuing twenty-eight years.

At Blackwater National Wildlife Refuge I asked biologist Roger Stone what he thought the chances were that a loblolly pine could survive in the Nanticoke cripples for more than two hundred years.

"There are so many variables," he said, shaking his head. "Any time a tree grows in a stressed environment like that it will be more susceptible to disease, and a taller tree, like a loblolly, is much more prone to lightning strikes. I don't think it's possible."

John Goslee and I are both in our seventies, and neither of us should any longer be struggling through the tangles and muck of the Nanticoke cripples, but Elija Wheedleton's grandson Mike is in the prime of life and relishes progging in all the wild reaches of the river. He has explored the cripples and visited the island several times and reports that no pines remain there that could possibly date to the early part of the nineteenth century.

I had all but closed the book on my investigation of Patty Cannon's Island when I was introduced to Lyle Gootee. Ruddy and now white-haired, Gootee grew up in Sharptown and spent his youth exploring the Nanticoke cripples whenever the opportunity presented itself. On one such outing he stumbled across a section of rusted chain, its links forged under the hammer of a blacksmith, and an iron ring on a bent wedge that also appears to be hand wrought. The artifacts lay on the ground, amidst the debris of a large, fallen and rotted pine tree. The ring had once been completely imbedded in its host and remains partially enclosed by the hard, knotty material that grew around it.

"They come from what we call Tick Island," Gootee explained. "Like you're coming from Sharptown and the first piece of high ground that sticks out in the river, that's it. It's before you get to the bend. There were big old pines in there then.

"I was just a kid when I got the ring and chain," Gootee continued. "It was in the [19]30s. Where I found them wasn't very far from the river. Of course things change. It used to be that from the time you got off the river—up in with the tuckahoes—you could walk to the island. It was sandy bottom then, but it ain't that way anymore. It's all mud now, clear out to the river."

Attaching no special significance to them, Gootee has saved the objects for sixty-five years. I was stunned when he offered them for my examination—the only physical evidence that I have seen to possibly support the legend of Patty Cannon's Island.

From their appearance and workmanship, the ring and chain could easily date to the first half of the nineteenth century or earlier—to the era of the kidnapping gang. What other purpose might they have served in such a forbidding place? Could someone have once secured livestock in that remote swamp, or were they utilized somehow in an early logging operation? I cannot answer the questions, and it is unlikely that anyone will ever document the origin and use of the artifacts with any certainty, but oh, the chill they send through me when I hold them in my hands.

The Ring and Chain from Tick Island

Shorter's Wharf

Carl Abbott's Light

I once heard a professional skeptic say that what we hope and fear and expect influences everything we see or think we see. That statement is, of course, undeniable, but many of us can recall an experience in which it fails to bring comfort.

Mysterious lights have been reported throughout history and are known by many names: will-o'-the-wisp, earth lights, jack-o-lanterns, jack-ma-jugs, spook or ghost lights to cite a few. These luminous orbs closely share our living space and should not be confused with the phenomena commonly referred to as UFOs.

To my knowledge, Nathaniel Crouch penned the earliest written American record of a "ghost light" in *The English Empire in America* (1685). "The Indians," he reported, "have a remarkable observation of flame that appears before the death of an Indian or English upon their wigwams in the dead of night; I was called out once about twelve a [sic] clock and plainly perceived it mounting into the air over a church. You may certainly expect a dead corpse in two or three days...."

Among numerous such preternatural occurrences reported in the United States, North Carolina's Brown Mountain Lights have probably received the most attention, baffling onlookers for more than two centuries. While a few still hold to the belief of early

109

frontiersmen that the dazzling array is a manifestation of the spirits of Cherokee and Catawba warriors slain in an ancient battle on the mountainside, most continue to search for a more practical explanation.

Gerard Will de Brahm, a German engineer, offered the first "scientific" theory in 1771. "The mountains," he conjectured, "emit nitrous vapors which are borne by the wind and when laden winds meet each other the niter inflames, sulphurates and deteriorates."

An investigation conducted by the United States Geological Survey on Brown Mountain in 1913 ignored the fact that the spectacle had been observed since the eighteenth century and concluded that locomotive headlights in the Catawba Valley were responsible. This claim was firmly discredited three years later when a severe flood knocked out the railroad bridges, roads and all electricity in the valley but failed to deter the appearance of the lights.

In an article in 1962 the Charlotte Observer published a local group's report that recalled de Brahm's 1771 theory by describing the discovery of a sweet-smelling gas that "ignites as it spurts through rock layers and burns with an orange glow." As with all previous investigations, however, the report ignored several major inconsistencies between its thesis and the actual manifestation of the lights, and few are satisfied today that the mystery has been solved.

Explanations offered for numerous similar phenomena across our continent include ball lightning; ignited methane gas from swamps and marshes; natural organic luminescence, such as fox fire; lights from automobiles, trains or airplanes; lights from towns or homesteads reflected from a sort of projection screen created where warm air currents meet cold air; fireflies and radioactive rocks or luminous energy created by a subterranean process—some sort of sub-atomic particle reaction caused by strain on the earth's tectonic plates.

Other persistent luminous phenomena that have received national recognition include the Maco light, also in North Carolina; the Marfa lights of West Texas; the Cahoke light at West Point, Virginia; the Gourdon light near Little Rock, Arkansas; the Yakima lights in

Washington State and others in South Carolina, Georgia, Kentucky, Oklahoma, Kansas, Illinois, Minnesota, Wisconsin and elsewhere.

Near Crisfield, Maryland, some older residents still speak of "Elsie's light." Elsie lived in a small house on a now deserted marsh until her residence caught fire one night and Elsie herself, it is said, became engulfed by flames. "For years and years," an informant reports, "you could see it of a night—her runnin' down to the water, all afire."

Maryland's Eastern Shore made larger headlines in the 1960s when observers lined up at dusk along Old Railroad Road, south of Route 50, hoping to catch a glimpse of Hebron's ghost light. "It stopped when they paved the road," a resident informed me.

Another Maryland apparition that is not widely known, though once observed by many, frequents marshes along the Blackwater River in South Dorchester County, usually in the vicinity of Shorter's Wharf and the small community of Robbins.

"I trapped down there and I've looked for it," Dave Robbins told me, "but I can't say I ever saw it. I was going around the corner of this fence one morning to fish my traps; it was five o'clock and it was dark. I looked, and there was a light. I didn't want to see it and I looked away. I said, 'Oh, it's just a firefly,' but it was March. When I got down around the corner, I looked back, but it wasn't there anymore. I can't really say what it was."

While Robbins is not certain that he ever saw the light, he introduced me to several people who speak with conviction about its existence.

Like Dave Robbins, Crawford Abbott grew up in the marshes along Blackwater River, and the two men now live on the same street in Cambridge. Crawford was working in his garage when Dave introduced us, and I asked him to tell me what he knew about the light.

"As far as I know," Abbott began, "it all started with my grandfather Carl Abbott. He was the first one to see it. Way back, I used to hear them say it would come out and pitch on your windowsill. They said that before Arthur [Abbott] died. I was only five years old then, and all I knew was a light was a light. It could have been or it could never been, but they said they saw it.

"My people are said to have seen it all their life, but I lived down there, and after I moved up here, I still went down there, and I never, ever, saw a light. It wasn't that I thought they was lying to me, but I had to take their word for it. I've been down there at four or five in the morning—all hours of the day—and never saw nothing.

"But then in October one year, me and my father were baiting ponds. We started baiting in October and we baited on Wednesday and weekends. It come Wednesday and I got off work and went on down the country. I picked my father up, which he lived down there then. We got a bag of corn and went on through the woods into my place and baited up all around the pond and come back. At that time of the year—in October—it gets dark early. It was sundown, near about, when we went down there, and we had to hurry to see where we were going.

"So we come on back to the field, and just as we turned out, there was two car tracks there. I was walking the left-hand one and my father was walking the right-hand one, and you know how you are when you're walking: You're looking around.

"One of my relatives had lived over in the woods not far—a great aunt and great uncle—but the house had burned down. I looked over there and I saw a light. I really didn't pay a whole lot of attention to it, but I walked another hundred or hundred and fifty feet and I said, 'I'd better say something to my father.' I looked at him and I said, 'I want to ask you something. Do you see a light over there?'

"He looked at me and he said, 'Yeah, I do.'

"So we kept our eye on it, and I'll tell you what it did: It made goose pimples run all over me. I could feel them coming up on my arm, and I ain't a scared person. I never, ever, thought it was going to hurt me, but it just give me that feeling.

"The road didn't go up to the house; it went maybe a hundred and fifty, two hundred yards by it at the closest point. So I walked a little bit and kept my eye on it. It never moved—never moved or blinked. It was a yellow, kerosene lantern looking thing. It was yellowish, like it was a kerosene light. I made up my mind I was gonna walk over there a little closer to it. There was a good-sized pond in between, and when I got up there and stopped, it was gone.

"We made excuses for it. Tonging [for oysters] starts down there in Fishing Bay in October, and my father said, 'Oh, it's probably a light on the bow of somebody's boat in the bay.' I said, 'Yeah, you're probably right.'

"So we went down there the next night just to find out if we could see Fishing Bay from where we were standing. About four years before that a man bought the piece of property joining my aunt's. It caught afire and burnt all the timber out, and a new growth of pine had come into it, and you know how they are when they come up—thick as they can be. We went down and stood there before dark, and there was no way in this God's world you could see through them pines to Fishing Bay to save your life. That's the first and only time that I seen anything that to me was unexplainable, but it made a believer out of me.

"They called the light a token of death and we always looked for something to happen after that, but it didn't relate to anything that happened at all.

"My grandfather died two years before I was born, so I didn't get to know him. He's the one that used to tell my father about the light. They all swore by it. I heard them talk about it so much. Some of them said it moved around and some said it would take off and go to a westerly direction. My grandfather told my father that sometimes it went so fast it had a tail behind it. When I saw it, it just disappeared before my eyes.

"When my older brother died, they said there was lights in the field where we lived, and some of them come up and was almost on the windowsill. They didn't just say a light; they said lights. The night before he died is when they all said that they saw the lights."

Evelyn Robinson, often referred to as the "Grand Dame of Dorchester," has lived near the marshes for all of her eight decades. "Like many families," she told me, "we had a graveyard in back of our house. It was a tremendous graveyard for that time; at least twenty-five people were buried in it. They were the older graves— brick vaults with a big marble slab—and many of them had elaborate tombstones. There would be lights there, and people said it was ghosts and tokens, but my grandmother explained to us children early in life that this was gas from the graves or from the marsh.

"I was coming across the marsh from work one foggy night and I saw a light. I remembered what my grandmother always told me: 'There is nothing to be afraid of. There is always an explanation.' But as I drove, that light really began to get to me; I really and truly began to believe what people had said, and it wasn't a very good feeling, especially in the fog. Then I came over the Shorter's Wharf Bridge and broke out of the fog. What I had been seeing was a security light.

"But years and years ago my daughter married a young man from Robbins, and his mother and all her family were firm believers that these lights meant that someone was going to die. My son-in-law's mother told me one day that she had seen this light. Her mother was elderly and she was thinking her mother would be the person to die. She was quite upset about it, but that weekend, she, herself, was killed in a tragic automobile accident.

"As a little girl I was at the old steamboat wharf [Wingate on the Honga River]. My father was a part of the seafood operation there. They would call out: 'So and so's coming in,' and you would go out and get ready to unload their seafood. One day they said, 'Ed Bradford's coming in. He's going very slow. He's towing something.' When they went out and looked over, Mr. Ed Bradford had a dead man. The man had come up to the surface and Mr. Bradford had put a rope around his legs.

"They had a telephone there and they immediately called the sheriff's office, but I don't remember the sheriff coming. They tried to identify the man but they could not do it. They figured that he had either fallen off one of the boats bringing in bootleg whiskey or off one of the steamboats and no one missed him. This was about 1929, and no one ever came forth to claim that body.

"Crab meat cans came in great big wooden boxes then. They were about an inch thick and about four foot wide and six foot long. My father and another man used some crab can boxes to build a coffin, and they buried this man on the point, right there on the river bank. After the old steamboat wharf was destroyed in [the hurricane of] 1933, my father went down to see if the grave had washed away.

"Years later, Mr. Ed Bradford's daughter told me a story. She said that her father was out in Honga River and Chesapeake Bay one day and fog came in. Every waterman—no matter how brave you are—is scared of fog. You have all this new technology today, but most watermen didn't even have a compass then. This fog came in so bad and so deep that he couldn't see anything. She said he was petrified. Just about the time he was giving up, thinking 'I'm gonna be hit by a ship out here,' a light came on his boat, and he followed that light until his boat hit bank. He took out a sounding pole and tied his boat—made her fast—and the light was still there. He got off and kept following that light until eventually he realized where he was. He was on his way home and everything was fine. So the next morning he said, 'Well, I've got to go search for my boat now.' He started backtracking, and when he found the boat, it had stopped next to that man's grave."

Brice Stump began his journalistic career in high school, and as a reporter and photographer for *The Daily Times* in Salisbury, Maryland, he has probably done more than any other individual to preserve the heritage of Delmarva's small communities.

At a discussion of his books one evening in the Dorchester County Public Library, Stump shared his encounter with the marsh light. "It's the only thing—if you want to call it the supernatural—that I have ever seen," he told the group. "I did see that light at Bestpitch Ferry [about five miles across the marsh from Shorter's Wharf], and it zipped right on down the marsh. Having grown up in the area, I knew there was nothing that could be going across the marsh that fast, that low. It was impossible for a boat and too low for an airplane. When I saw it, I knew immediately what it was."

Stump suggests that the light may date back to the Civil War and may have played a part in Harriet Tubman's success in guiding slaves from the area on her Underground Railroad. "I believe that people were reluctant to pursue her at night because of the presence of the light," Stump said.

Inez North Abbott Travers told me she was born at Robbins, "But I left when I was a baby," she quickly added. "My father was a farmer, and there was no tillable land much at Robbins. He started buying farmland, and whenever he bought a new farm, we moved there." Most of George North's property was in the Drawbridge District and Griffith Neck, along the Chicamacomico River, and it was there that his daughter spent her formative years.

I asked Miss Inez when the light was first observed. "I was sixteen years old when I moved back to Robbins," she replied. "It was a nice little town, so thickly settled then, and people kept their homes up. I knew nobody there except my grandmother, but I soon made friends. The light had been seen, but I was young and paying lights no mind. I was sixteen then and I'm ninety-one now.

"My husband's father was the first one ever saw it. I would say that was back maybe in 1915 or 1916. Some called it the 'marsh light' and some called it 'Kyle's light.'"

Miss Inez's first husband was Arthur Abbott, now deceased, and his father was Carl Abbott. Everyone I have met from Robbins agrees that Carl was the first to see the light, but they consistently pronounce his name as "Kyle" when referring to the light.

"The first time Mr. Abbott saw it," Inez continued, "he was paddling down the river one pretty moonshiny night. He could paddle a skiff and never make a wave in the water—never make a noise. The wild ducks didn't pay him no mind, and he could get so close to them. Oh, he was a hunter. He hunted, hunted, and he fished, fished, fished.

"When he wanted to go hunting, he would go in the yard and call the live decoys: 'Quack, quack, quack,' on a duck call. You could use live decoys at that time. Then he'd set down on one knee and the ducks would jump on his other knee. He'd put them in his bag and take his gun and off he'd go.

"Mr. Abbott owned a lot of marsh, and the light played in his marsh. When he'd come back from hunting, the first thing they'd ask: 'Well, Pop, did you see the light?' 'Well, yes' or 'Well, no,' he'd say. It didn't appear every night.

"It's a graveyard back there called Sandy Hill. Almost all the people from Robbins is buried in there, all of my husband's people and my father and Granny Anna [Anna Robbins, who died in 1928 at the age of 105]. It was an old cedar about the middle of the graveyard, and the light liked to be around that old cedar.

"It always puzzled me quite a lot, but it seemed that after we'd see the light, it wouldn't be too long before somebody would be buried in there. Well, not every time, but it didn't miss too many. All the people over there liked to say they saw the light. It was quite a sight—an experience to see it—but they didn't like to know that somebody probably would die.

"My husband traveled in the marsh and he saw the light quite a lot. I was always digging roots [family history] up, and I asked him one day about the first time he saw the light. He told me he was duck hunting down in a pond on the marsh. There was another graveyard not too far from where he was and it was called 'Wroten's.' He was out there by hisself when the light come. He said he didn't feel too good when he seen it coming; it was coming straight for him. He was nothing but a youngster then. He said he jumped in the pond and went down in the mud and water and just left his nose out, and he nearly froze. He said he really got frightened. He said it come directly over that pond and went bump and bump a-round in that pond. He said he thought it never would leave, but finally it did. When he got out, he was mud more than anything else, and cold. He started running, and he had a right good ways to run to his boat. He said, 'If I hadn't had my gun in my hand—if I had laid her down—I'd have never stopped to pick her up. He said when he got to that boat, he jumped into her and left the live de-coys. He said, 'I went home and the ducks stayed all night.' And they were anchored, the ducks were.

"One time I saw it, we were coming across the marsh road and we were driving slow. It was a pretty moonshiny night. It was a Saturday and we had been in town. My husband said to me, 'You know, it's a nice night to see the light, isn't it?' I said, 'Yeah, I'd love to see it tonight.' And we looked and seen it on the graveyard, and then it come across the river on the marsh side. When it would come, it would bounce, just to the marsh tops. Sometimes it was

117

fast, and when it did go fast, it would go almost like a streak of lightning. It come almost to our car. It was on the marsh but good enough that you could see it, and we stopped the car. It was right good size. I'll say it would remind you more or less of a pumpkin, a good-sized pumpkin, and it was the color.

"People came for miles to try and see the light. My brother-in-law was a preacher and he lived in Pennsylvania. He wanted to see the light and he took a chance. I told him it would always come to the cemetery first, and I told him where the graveyard was and to drive slow. He came across the marsh and he saw it. He said it come out to the road and got to his back fender of the car—close to it—and trailed him right to the bridge, and then it disappeared. He was a-panting when he came. He said, 'I'm glad I saw it, but it was something to see.'"

In George Carey's *A Faraway Time and Place—Lore of the Eastern Shore*, I discovered this paragraph: "In Dorchester County 'Cal's Light' has, over the years, gained notoriety as a death omen. Reputedly, on first sighting, the light popped up beside a waterman's boat and when he passed his hand through the flame it disappeared. Somewhat later, the same light appeared outside his home during the evening, and the following day he perished. Since that time, the light has appeared outside other nearby homes, and on each occasion someone within has died in the next several days."

I have no doubt that "Cal's light" is a reference to the same phenomenon as Carl Abbott's or "Kyle's" light. I told Carey's story to Miss Inez and she replied without hesitation: "That was Arthur's brother, Wilson, but the story isn't quite accurate. Wilson was with the marine police force, and he developed a serious illness and had to come home. It wasn't the night he came home, but the light came and pitched right on the bow of his boat and set there awhile. In a day or two he got worse, and he died in a week's time."

Corbett Robbins was born and continues to live in the now diminished community of Robbins. Like most of the old timers, he once made his living from the bounty of the marshes. "I bought fur down there," he proudly informed me. "I bought in three states, and I shipped 20,000 muskrat hides every two or three weeks."

Corbett's lungs are crippled by emphysema, and he carries an oxygen tank with him to assist his breathing. "I done it to myself," he admits, with reference to smoking cigarettes, a habit he has not entirely abandoned. At times it is an effort for this elderly gentleman to speak, but his eyes sparkle when you mention the light.

"I don't know of nobody that seen the light in the last fifteen or twenty years," he began [some place the last sighting closer to forty years ago], "and I've looked for it too. I last seen it back on that shore, back in the '60s. Where it's at now, I don't know, but it definitely was there.

"I don't know what it was—if it was light from gasses coming up from the marshes. But it don't make no sense that it was marsh gasses. It would pitch up trees, and mysterious things would happen where you see it at. It acted like it had a mind on it because it would come to you. I just don't know.

"It hung around on the graveyard a lot, but it's a mystery about the thing. You got people down there that lived right on that graveyard and said they never seen it in their life. And there's a Wroten graveyard back there, and that's where it seems like it originated.

"Most times, people seen it back in the marshes. It was very active in the '30s and the '40s. How far it goes back from there, I don't know. It varied in size and it would bounce. It would be that big sometimes [he curved his hands and held them to the size of a basketball], but if it come towards you, it would get smaller.

"I know one man said he seen it, and he was a reliable old man—Al Garcia. He was always out in them marshes back in the '30s and the '40s. He was on his way to his boat one time during the lightning bugs, and he said it passed him on the path. It had a light like a lightning bug; I mean it was a color of the lightning bug, a fluorescent color light most of the time. It was on his boat, but he couldn't let the light stop him.

"The last time I seen it, I was on the shore. Me and a bunch of us was down there, and it come towards the car. It come through the fog and come around to the back. It was floating back there a right good time. It wasn't no bigger than that [he shaped his fingers to the size of a baseball] when it got to the car. I got upset and thought, 'Well, that thing's after me,' and I got out of there. They said they looked back, and everything back there was lit up.

"I didn't see it that many times. I seen it three times all my life. Fog was a time it showed up, or a snowstorm. One time my father seen it, it was a snowstorm.

"My father seen it about two mile down in the marsh one night, and it come right to him. It followed him clear on up through the marsh, followed him clear up through the woods. That was it, and he come on home. But he was scared of it, I'll tell you that. People were scared of it, no doubt about that.

"I've heard that after people seen it, somebody would die. I don't know that, but the light was there. It was no doubt about a light being there."

Sandy Hill Cemetery

Rest Well, Mr. Flat

There is an old Eastern Shore adage that says: "Pick a rainy day to bury somebody and their spirit will go to heaven." On the day we buried J. Granville Hurst, heaven wept all morning long.

I first met Granville on another stormy day in April 1972, when I purchased my little farm at an auction in Vienna. Sheets of wind-driven rain had made the announced location of the sale—the bank steps—much too uncomfortable, and the auctioneer requested permission to move to the overhang of what I understood was "Flathurst's Station." It took a month or so for me to discover that he had really said, "Flat Hurst's station."

My first conversation with Mr. Flat was in a nearby country store. He and two old friends—one, a graying beagle—had been out for a ride and stopped to visit. He gave me his recipe for catfish that afternoon, and I decided that Granville Hurst was somebody I wanted to know.

When the old beagle eventually became totally disabled, Mr. Flat sadly carried her to a veterinarian to end her suffering. "She went to sleep smilin'," he told me and then added, "I hope I can go that easy." On June 4, 2001, at the age of eighty-seven, his wish was granted.

Mr. Flat told me a story once about a colorful character whose diverse talents included singing, praying and cussing. "Man," my informant emphasized, "Alban could pray somethin' wicked, and he could cuss somethin' wicked."

When an old woman died, Alban was drafted to serve as pallbearer. It was the first funeral at which the undertaker used a then new device to automatically lower the coffin into the grave instead of using ropes and manual labor.

When the mortician pressed a button and the casket slowly began to sink into the earth, Alban looked on for a minute, then muttered, "Old lady, I don't know what kind of a damn time you had comin' into this world, but damn if you ain't goin' away easy."

I don't know what kind of a time my friend Granville had coming into this world, but all of his friends are grateful that his exit came swiftly and easily, after a long and useful life, and that it came while he was doing what he did best—being a friend and helper in his community.

Granville Hurst was born on October 28, 1913, at Ravenwood Farm in Dorchester County, where his parents lived with his grandfather—a sharecropper.

"Times were hard when I was comin' up and we were poor," Flat told me, "but we had plenty to eat. A woman asked me one time what we ate then. I told her we ate beans and salt fish and bread.

"She said, 'Well, I couldn't eat no beans.'

"I said, 'The hell you can't, if you're hungry.'"

Around the age of seven, Flat moved to town with his parents and eventually became his father's partner in the service station. Except for European duty in an artillery battalion during World War II, he remained in the business for fifty years.

"How did you get the nickname?" I once asked him. Several people to whom I had posed the question had no idea. He had been called "Flat" for as long as they could remember.

"I started changin' tires when the Model-A Ford came out," he replied, "and I was pretty good at it, so they started callin' me 'Flat.' As many tires as I've changed in my life, if I'd had the price they charge now for repairin' one, I'd be a millionaire."

Mr. Flat always had a tale to tell, and like the wonderful old sages who once provided community entertainment from their benches in the country stores, he knew how to spin a yarn. If you sat for a spell on his porch or went for a drive with Flat, the stories poured out of him like a surging tide. Every mention of a name, a place, a subject, and every bend in the road or creek brought back a flood of memories to a mind that never lost its edge.

If you encountered Mr. Flat only briefly in the post office or the bank or on one of his many errands around town, you always came away with at least a smile. The last time we met, I dropped a hasty comment about the recent lack of rain and learned that the current drought wasn't nearly as bad as one the region had suffered years ago. "It was so dry that time," my informant offered with a wry grin, "that the baby catfish down at Savannah Lake were six months old before they learned how to swim."

The last words we exchanged were an agreement to take a ride again real soon. There were stories he wanted to tell me, and I was anxious to hear them.

Perhaps the greatest tribute I can pay to Mr. Flat is to share a few of his words on these pages and preserve them for at least a little while longer. Here is a fragment of what I learned from him on one spring drive:

"These people from here on down were real country folks. I'm not makin' light of them, now. People in town thought they were corny because they had no education and they never had been any place but here, but they had a load of wisdom.

"This house used to be a country school. They had one every so many miles along this road—just small, one-room schools. You didn't need a college education to teach back then. Matter of fact, some taught without even a high-school education.

"I quit school when I was fifteen, almost sixteen years old, and went to work for my father and his brother. They had the hardware store and the station, and they had a wood yard too. Everybody burned wood then and the schools burned wood.

"There were so many country schools that the board of education accepted bids on who would supply the cordwood to 'em. My father and his brother had the contract with all the schools in this area. They'd each order six or seven or eight cords of oak and a couple cords of pine slab to start the fire with. I hauled a mess of wood to these schools.

"A fellow found some gold down there in the Weston Mansion one time—they said he did. He donated the money to build a church here, so they named it after him—Wainright's Chapel. A little bit of money looked awful big in those days. The buildin's gone now, but they had big revivals here. People would tie their boat up at Lewis Wharf and they'd walk up here—come in the mornin' and stay all day.

"After you get past the crossroads, scarcely anybody lives down here now, but when I was growin' up, man, people lived in the bushes everywhere.

"A store set here. People walked for miles just to sit on an old nail keg and chew tobacco and eat peanuts and tell some lies. Years ago the little stores used to stay open till nine or ten o'clock at night. They didn't sell a damn thing. People just sat around and made a mess—eat peanuts and throwed their shells on the floor—and they told stories. They told some terrible tales.

"These roads were bad when I was young. If you went for a ride in a Model-T and got back home without bein' stuck, you thought you really accomplished somethin'. You might have one of the early automobiles, but in the wintertime you used horses—drove horses to a carriage.

"A man was talkin' one time about how muddy this road used to be. He said he come along here one day and saw a hat layin' in the road. It was a nice-lookin' hat, so he picked it up, and there was a man's head under there. He said to the man, 'Mister, you in bad shape, ain't you?'

"'Nope,' the man said, 'I'm just fine, but my old hoss ain't doin' too good down there.'

"An old guy told me once about the first automobile he ever saw. He lived way down below here on an island. The only way he could get to school when he was a boy, he had to have a boat, and then he had to walk several miles. So he was walkin' up here one day and he heard this noise comin' down the road. He didn't know what in the world that thing was, so he hid in the bushes till it got by.

"There was this one old man down here who was real eccentric. He was a nice old fellow but he was very particular. He bought a power garden tractor one time, and that was a big thing back then. Of course it was tore up more than it would work, I'm sure of that. But anyway, he lost a bolt out of it, and he was down to the store just a-worryin' hisself to death. The boys told him, 'Oh, hell, Captain Cal, don't worry about it. Just take a piece of pine and whittle it down a little and drive it right in there.'

"'No sir,' he said. 'The man [who] made her put a bolt in there, and be damned if I ain't gonna put a bolt in there.'

He finally found one.

"Levin lived here. He wasn't very tidy. If he liked you, he'd do anything in the world for you, but if he didn't—stay out of his way. He was a right good mechanic on old-time cars, but with the modern ones, now, he'd be handicapped. He never told you his business and he didn't ask you any of yours. Like the preacher who preached at his funeral said, he was a level-land hillbilly. He made his own laws and he lived by 'em. What he thought was right, he did. He didn't go to church but he was a good-hearted man.

"Long John lived here, a great, tall man. His name was Hughes. He used to cultivate some of this land with oxen, but he couldn't live off the land—it was just too poor. Now it's full of salt and won't even grow timber—maybe pulp wood on the high spots. His son Lawrence shot the first deer anybody saw around these parts in my time. We never had deer when I was growin' up. I think Colonel duPont let that buck go, and it come on up this way.

"Some fairly good timber grew on the islands below here. They had an upright boiler with a great big winch on it and a cable. They'd put the boiler right up on the road here and drag the cable back into the island with a mule and hook it onto the logs. The man at the boiler pulled a lever, and it would wind 'em right in. They call it snakin' 'em out. An old friend of mine used to snake all those trees out, but he's dead and gone now.

"There was good land at Savanna Lake years ago but it's sunk-

126

en and full of salt now. They grew fine tomatoes in there. We had three canneries in Vienna then.

"George Richardson used to cut marsh grass with a sickle mower and two mules out on this marsh. Then they would bale it and ship it to Baltimore. They used to pack china in it.

"I never told nobody about it 'cause I didn't want nobody messin' at it, but I had a place right on this deep bend on the creek. I caught some nice perch in there, but the last couple of years it hasn't been anything. I think it's the damned old nutrias. Way back there, a fellow that owned a lot of marsh went down to Louisiana to that muskrat skinnin' contest, and they were tellin' him about how good eatin' the nutrias were and how they sold the fur. He had eight or ten pair shipped up to him, and he let 'em go in the marsh. Damn! That was the worst thing in the world he could ever do. They're everywhere now and they tear the marsh all to pieces.

"A family of Grays lived in a big house right in there, and they owned a lot of marsh. It was three or four brothers of 'em trapped. Years ago, when muskrats were five dollars apiece for just the pelts, they used to catch five thousand rats. That was a fortune then, but the prices got right down to nothin'."

And so, mile after mile, Mr. Flat's narration went on. Volumes of knowledge recorded only in the mind of this amazing man. As we crossed the bridge onto Elliott Island, he said, "I came down here one time with my father when he sold cars for a Ford agency. He sold a Model-T tourin' car, and I went with him to deliver it. This man's name was Fred Ewell. We went in the kitchen and got the papers straight, and then Mr. Fred said to his wife, 'Bring some of that money out here.' And damn if he didn't pay for that Model-T with quarters, fifty-cent pieces and silver dollars."

In her eulogy, the Reverend Mary Ann Farnell said, "He is survived by one son, two grandsons, two nephews and a whole community of adopted family. He had his loving family, but he belonged to all of us, too. He gave his heart to everyone. Such a humble and honest and decent man he was. I will venture to say he has probably knocked on every door in this community with something in his hand. He was generous as well."

127

As we looked on his father's earthly remains for one final time, Steve Hurst turned to me and said, "A whole library is gone."

And indeed it is—a whole library that can never be written.

Rest well, Mr. Flat.

J. Granville Hurst

Thank You
for Calling Horizon

I usually write about Delmarva's special people and the peninsula's wonderfully rich history and lore, but this is going to be a telephone tale.

Although every word that you are about to read is true (and there are many more words that I don't have the space to print here, along with a few that my editor would surely censor), I am going to change the name of the industry in question, a megacorporation that expresses pride in one of its slogans: "We give more than our word; we give our worry-free guarantee." I'll call the company "Horizon" in honor of that intangible line that sits way out in the distance, which moves whenever you do and can never be reached.

The event that precipitated this narrative began simply enough: I couldn't get on the Internet one morning. For one hour and thirty minutes I wore my computer mouse to a frazzle by clicking on "connect," time after time after time. With each cricket-like snap, a lady's monotone voice informed me that "We're sorry, but all circuits are busy."

This frustration had been repeated at intervals of a month or so for more than a year. If I persistently worked the mouse, I could usually succeed in achieving a contact within five or ten minutes, but sometimes the failure persisted for hours, and at times the condition extended intermittently over a period of several days.

I had complained before to my server, a Delmarva company with a local telephone number, whose manager informed me that Horizon had a foul-up in some cable box in West Ocean City, and though it had been discussed with them on many occasions, Horizon had done nothing to correct it. He was unable to explain how a defect in Ocean City could target me, forty-five miles away, but I have come to understand that distance is little more than a mental perception in the twenty-first century. The last time my neighbor reported an electric power failure, which had darkened several miles of our countryside, a man in Minnesota informed her that everything looked just fine on the panel in front of him.

So on the morning in question I decided to call the alleged source of the problem and add my name to what I assumed must by now be a long list of angry customers. After working my way through the plethora of recorded menus to reach a live voice, the voice bluntly informed me that Horizon does not guarantee Internet connections. I asked to speak to a supervisor and was told that somebody would get back to me within two hours.

I'm going to do a flashback here and tell you that this was not my first encounter with Horizon. Several weeks prior to the Internet problem, I thought it strange for two days that every time I responded to my ringing telephone, all I heard was an annoying noise. To conserve space, I shall dispense with the discovery process and simply inform you that the sound was a fax machine attempting to communicate with me. My telephone number and the number of someone's fax had been interchanged; when people called me, they got the fax machine, and when one of its kind attempted to send a message to the appliance with my number, my phone rang. Horizon was unable to correct the problem on the day that it was discovered but agreed to forward all calls to the correct terminals until they could.

They didn't.

Prior to that incident I had picked up my telephone receiver one day and was greeted by silence. I immediately plugged a phone into the junction box outside to see if it was an internal or external problem. The terminal was dead, so I called repair from a friend's house. Would you believe that there are people working in Horizon's repair department who do not know that there is a junction box on the outside of my house?

After a five-minute struggle with two ladies to make myself understood, I learned that my telephone number had accidentally been reassigned to someone else. After four days of frustrating encounters with a variety of Horizon employees, I was told that everything had been corrected.

Not quite! I soon discovered that I had lost my caller ID in the process, and that required additional communication and days of waiting.

By the end of the ordeal I had spoken to more than a dozen Horizon employees, some helpful and some helpless. The one consistency I noted was that each of them signed off with a mechanically delivered "Thank you for calling Horizon."

Sometime later, when my caller ID stopped functioning again, I assumed the device was broken, but when a newly purchased model also drew a blank, I returned to searching the menus.

"Well, that's a bummer," a man at Horizon said when I told him that I had needlessly purchased a second device. I was informed that it was a business office problem and was promised a call back, which never came, but service was mysteriously restored a day later.

Then, several weeks afterward, a friend told me that someone else's name was registering on his ID every time I rang. Space does not permit a review of that episode, so back to the story I began to tell.

The callback in response to my Internet problem had failed to arrive in the promised two hours and I needed to run some errands. When I returned, there was a message on my answering machine. More correctly, it was a conversation between two Horizon employees who had been chatting while connected to my open line.

I worked my way through the menus again and requested a supervisor. When a man responded, I asked, "Are you a supervisor?"

"No," he replied after a brief hesitation.

When I *insisted* on speaking to a supervisor, I was put on hold and entertained by a long musical interlude until a woman's voice greeted me.

"May I ask your name?" I said.

"My name is Miss Ross, supervisor on duty."

I took a deep breath, relaxed, and calmly explained everything that I had suffered at the hands of Horizon during the past year. Then I asked Miss Ross to be patient for another minute and listen to the partial conversation on my answering machine. Let me remind you that this was in response to my complaint about the Internet connection.

"Uh huh," the tape began.

"Well, that's not their number, so why it's in the system under their number—their name—I don't know. But [someone else's name, address and number]...."

"It must been their old number, and now Hal Roth has it."

"Yeah, must be. Did you say Roth—R-o-t-h?"

"Uh huh. Hal Roth."

"Yeah, I see it. I don't, uh...."

"He's at [my address]. He was the one I talked to."

"Yeah, uh, you talked to Roth?"

"Yes, but you know, I thought I had said [someone else's name]. Maybe I...."

"Yeah, well, you said [someone else's name]."

"I understood Hal; last name is Hal."

"Oh, see, I...."

"I'm not sure but that's the last or first name."

"Ah, I don't know, cause I thought that's what she said when she answered the phone. She had said something like that, like a... a Hal or a something. I don't know. I don't see nothing. I don't see any Roths in the phone book, so...." (I *am* in the phone book, as are a number of other Roths.)

"Yeah, well, uh, it's Roth when you see the order that was done yesterday." (To my knowledge there was no order under my name the previous day.)

"Naw, I'm just looking in the phone book. I can't look in all that

133

mess."

"Aw, ha, ha, ha, ha."

"Uh, well, I don't know. I just talked to Miss [name]. She said they're not having any problems, so...."

"It's Hal Roth that's complaining."

"Oh, O.K. Now where does he live?"

"He lives at [my address]."

"Oh, O.K. Hold on—[my address]. O.K. Cause you gave me [someone else's address]."

"I know; that's what the line records show."

"O.K. O.K. [my address], and his name is Roth?"

"Hal Roth"

"And he is 376-2144?"

"Yeah."

"All right. So can we get the records straight?"

"You know what...."

"End of messages."

"Are you beginning to get a picture?" I asked Miss Ross.

"Hmmm. Yes, I am," she replied. "When I pull up your order, I see so many different names on the account. It's a business office problem. I'm going to get them on the line with us."

I held on—no music this time.

"O.K. I called the business office and got the number that they're supposed to have assigned. He gave me a totally different number than what it was. They have you crossed with [someone else's number]. The [someone else's name] just got a new service, and when they hooked it up, it crossed itself somehow. Their number is coming up as yours and yours is coming up as theirs. I'll go ahead and put a ticket in for this. The central office will get the lines uncrossed and also give you credit for every twenty-four hours that you have been out of service with these problems."

They haven't.

I thanked Miss Ross and asked how I might get back to her in case I encountered additional problems.

"Just call the repair department and ask for Miss Ross. There are seven offices located all over the country. I'm in the Denver office."

"Denver? Really? Well, how's the weather in Denver today?"

"It's sunny, but it was very rainy last night."

We shared our amazement at how the world works these days, and Miss Ross said, "I'll go ahead and send this through now. Thank you for calling Horizon."

An hour or two later my phone rang.

"This is Horizon calling; are you having problems with your telephone?"

"I've been having nothing but problems with my telephone for months now!"

"Well you don't have to get excited about it!"

"It's hard not to."

I uttered a great sigh, leaned back in my chair and went through the whole story once again, ending with another playing of the recording on my answering machine. While I held the mouthpiece to the recorder's speaker, the lady on the open line kept loudly calling my name; it was obvious that she did not want to hear the recording. With each of her shouts I pressed the mouthpiece closer to the speaker.

When "End of messages" sounded, I asked, "Are you beginning to understand a little of my frustration?"

"Wait a minute," the voice in my ear said. "The lady that was talking, is that who you were talking to in Denver?"

"No. The lady you just heard on my answering machine is someone who attempted to call me earlier in the day," and I reviewed the highlights again.

"Oh, she probably had him on the line and was trying to call you to see what was wrong. So... [someone else's number], is that your number?"

"No, my number is 2144."

"And you have no dial tone at times?"

"Where does that come from?

"It's on your repair order."

"That has not been part of my problem today, and I have not reported that to anybody at Horizon."

"Well, that's what's on the report."

I calmly reiterated the highlights.

"I have the number she put on there that the line is crossed with, but it's nowhere near your location, so I don't know how it could be crossed. Call me back. Let me give you my number so you can call me."

"Is that long distance?"

"Where are you?"

"In Vienna, Maryland."

"Yeah, it'll be long distance. I'll see that you get credit for the call."

She didn't.

I called the woman back and was informed that my line was not crossed with another. I thanked her and decided to speak again with Miss Ross.

"Thank you for calling Horizon," the woman said as she signed off.

I listened once more to the menus and selected the repair department. A man answered. "I would like to speak to Miss Ross in repair, please," I said.

"What's her extension?"

"She didn't give me an extension; she told me to call the repair department and ask for her by name."

"Well, we have seven different repair offices around the country."

"No problem," I shot back; "she's in Denver."

"Do you know the exchange out there?"

"It's your company; don't you know it?"

"I can't do anything without a number."

I heaved another sigh and gave a now much-practiced overview of my problem.

"There's a repair order out for your number," he replied.

"And what does it say?" I asked.

"Are you hearing other voices on your line when you're talking?"

"No, I am not hearing voices on my line. Where are you located?"

"Richmond."

"Please transfer me to a top-level supervisor; I am completely frustrated."

"Just a moment."

The music that Horizon plays while you're waiting is very calming, and I'm sure that was a major consideration when they selected it.

After several minutes the voice returned: "Thank you for your patience. There is no supervisor available at the moment but someone will call you within two hours."

"Does that come under your worry-free guarantee?"

There was silence on the other end of the line.

"A return call within two hours, is that a promise?" I asked.

"It's a promise. Thank you for calling Horizon."

One year, two months, three weeks, two days, eight hours and fifteen minutes of the promised two hours have now passed. My hand is cocked above my telephone receiver; I'm sure it's going to ring any second now.

On the same day that I was struggling to retain my sanity, 55,000 East Coast customers of Horizon's wireless pager division were opening bills that listed an 800 number to call for inquiries. Those who dialed the number were greeted by a recording that told them their call would cost $1.99 per minute and they should hang up immediately if they were under 18. That message was followed by a sultry female voice: "Welcome to Intimate Connections, where you'll hear sexy introductions from callers on our system right now. Talk only to the girls who turn you on. Send private uncensored messages or talk live one-on-one. To join the fun, press 1 now."

When Lloyd Grove, Washington Post staff writer, reached Jim Gerace, a Horizon company vice president, Gerace knew nothing of the mix-up. He later called back and said, "We regret the error. Because of your expert reporting, we were able to stop the issuing of further bills with the wrong number. We're not happy about this, and we're not going to be happy when we read your paper splashing it all over the place."

The next time you're bored and looking for adventure, call Verizon—oops—Horizon. They'll thank you for it.

Jimmy Simmons

138

Delmarva's
Pioneer Grocer

S hopping in the modern supermarket, where you can browse leisurely through aisles stacked with goodies, taking all the time you want to make selections of fresh produce, canned goods from home and abroad, a wide selection of meats and cheeses, drinks, dry goods—everything from milk to motor oil—has become such a normal and accepted routine that we older citizens have pretty much pushed aside the memories of how it was when we were growing up. And those under forty can't even imagine what grocery stores were like in the 1920s and '30s, when customers were waited on individually by the grocer and choices were slim.

Jimmy Simmons remembers. In Center Market on Race Street in Cambridge, Maryland, Jimmy was the pioneer who led Delmarva into the modern era of grocery merchandising.

"For ten years, from 1920 to 1930," Simmons told me as we sat one morning in the garden center next to Center Market, "I was in my daddy's store down on Hoopers Island. That got me started off in the store business. He was a contract carpenter and undertaker, and he had a store. And he was one of the few men on the island that could repair shoes. He did all that kind of stuff. I grew up in the store—W. A. Simmons, General Merchandise. It burned down about 1928.

"When I graduated, I come to Cambridge," Simmons continued to reminisce. "I had to. My mother did wrong. I saved a quantity of nickels and dimes. All they were in them days was just nickels and dimes and pennies. You got no quarters. You picked tomatoes for a nickel a basket, and you'd go out in the woods and get a million jiggers for a bucket of blueberries and blackberries. I did everything for to make some money, and I got enough to pay the down payment on a car. It was a crazy thing, which my mother should have never let me did. It was a beautiful thing, though, a yellow Chevrolet convertible with red wire wheels and side fenders. She had the works."

After seventy years the shine of that convertible still leaps from Simmon's eyes.

"I had to work," he continued in a sterner voice. "The payments was thirty-two dollars a month. I'll never forget 'em. So I come to Cambridge to work for ten dollars a week. That's forty dollars a month, and yet the payments was thirty-two. And the gasoline.... Things went along like that till 1937."

1937 was the year when Simmons bought his own store, directly across Race Street from where he had been working since 1930. Within another year the enterprising young man would be operating the first self-service grocery on Delmarva.

"I seen the need for a change in the grocery business after I read a piece in the paper. This little ad said they were thinking about changing the way they shopped at the old-time grocery stores and let people wait on their ownself. So my wife and I had a little flabjab there. 'Well,' I said to my wife, 'if they can do anything like that out West, we can do it right here in Dorchester County.' I owned the building then and I said, 'We'll take the partition out and operate for a while without self-service. Then we'll go in self-service.'

"Just recently we had a lady come up from the Maryland Grocery Association in Baltimore, and she says could I tell her some things about the early grocery shopping carts. I said, 'Yes, Ma'am. I can tell you they're like a folding chair made by a company in Indiana, but if you come down, I'll show you one of the first shopping carts of the new concept of self-service.' I said, 'I'll show you the first cart that was used south of Wilmington.' We had the first self-service store south of Wilmington, and it was very successful.

"I saved all that stuff," Simmons proudly announced. "Every week I'd put all the ads and all the promotions in a book I saved."

Simmons soon became president of the Maryland Retail Grocers' Association, where, he told me, "I was very political-minded as far as the store business was concerned."

He was also very innovative in merchandising.

"When we first opened our store in 1937, your mother and your daddy couldn't buy a chicken out of the case the way you can now. There were no dressed chickens in those days. You have to buy 'em live and take 'em home with you live. I put a sign out there the first weekend that I was open, and it said, 'Buy your chicken from me and I'll dress it free.' About the first hour on the first day I was out of chickens. I said, 'I won't be out next week; I'll buy double the amount.' And that's what I did.

"We were the first ones, and we sold so many chickens because the man across the street kept his old way of doing it. This old man come across the street and said, 'Jim, what are you doing here? You can't dress them chickens for nothing.' He said, 'I'm not gonna do it.'

"I worked for him for seven years and operated his store, and I knew I could make a success of it. I knew it! I said, 'Well, you do what you want to do. I'm not working for you no more; I'm working for my ownself.'

"He says, 'You can't do it.'

"I says, 'Yes, I can.' I said, 'Don't you see them feathers floating around in here. My mother's in the back room right now dressing chickens, and she ain't gonna charge me nothing because I don't charge her nothing to keep her.' So I said, 'We're gonna keep on doing it.'

"The old man said, 'Well, I'm not gonna do it,' and he didn't do it.

"I'd been there for seven years, and I knew that all he sold was four or five crates of chickens a week. Well, what happened was this: I had doubled my order, and I run out of chickens again and

141

was taking orders for the next week, and he still had them four crates of chickens. It got so we were selling so many chickens I had to build a chicken house in back of the store.

"I invented a chicken picker a long time before Perdue was ever thought of. I had made this out of a drum, and I put an axle in the middle of it and hooked a motor up to it. I drawed little squares—about two-inch squares—and made a checkerboard all the way around that drum. This took some time, and where every place crossed, I drilled holes and run a bolt from the inside up through the holes. It had a screw on it. Then I went up to Charley Mace's bicycle shop and bought a whole roll of tricycle tire that had wire in the middle of it. Well, I cut it in pieces and pulled that wire out and screwed it down on that bolt and let it stick up. That was something to see—rubber fingers all the way around that drum.

"This guy Isaac had been working for me a long while, and he eyed that thing up. He didn't think much of it. I said, 'Isaac, let me show you something here. I want to show you how to work this thing.'

"'Mr. Jimmy,' he said, 'do you got to do that?'

"I said, 'You're gonna have to do it. You're the one taking care of the chicken house, ain't you?' So I said, 'Try it now.'

"He tried it, and it worked pretty good for him, but he didn't want to get too close to it. I said, 'O.K., you can dress this cooker full of chickens. You got something here now that really works.'

"The first one he tried—he knocked on the back door. I was cutting up some pork chops and I went and looked. He said, 'Mr. Jimmy, I done somethin'.'

"I said, 'What you mean, Isaac?'

"He said, 'I really messed this chicken up.'

"He held it up and it didn't have neither piece of skin in the world. He left it in the water too hot, too long, and them rubber tips was firm. They hadn't worked themselves too soft yet, and he skinned it. It was the funniest looking thing you ever seen.

"And then I went and left that chicken picker outside and let the rust eat it out for years. I am so sorry I didn't keep it because it actually worked and worked fine.

"Well, we got so we had a chicken sale—ninety-five cents or ninety-eight cents for a whole chicken, all dressed. People lined up, and one of 'em says, 'Can't you have 'em in an ice case, all covered with ice?'

"Then old Mary says, 'Mr. Jimmy, could you cut that chicken up for me. I don't see very good.'

"I said, 'Yeah, Mary, come on.'

"And she come back to me where I was cutting it up, and the first thing I cut off was a wing. 'Oh,' she says, 'I do love them things. I never get all I can eat of wings.' And when I took the gizzard and put it in a little package, she said, 'There's another thing I love. I never get enough gizzards.'

"So that give me another idea, and I said, 'Mary, you come back next Thursday afternoon and I'll sell you all the chicken wings you want.'

"That was the beginning of cut-up chicken. Mary was the first woman to have cut-up chicken. I put a sign in the window: 'Buy only the parts you like best.'

"They'd come in and say, 'Mr. Jimmy, do you mean I can buy all the legs I want?'

"I said, 'Sure.'

"We were the first on many occasions, being the first to offer new things to the people. We were the first to have gallon jugs of milk. I went to Lewes, Delaware—Lewes Dairy. He said yes, he'd be glad to come down to Cambridge. I think you had to order about five hundred gallons to start with. It was a tremendous success—gallon jugs of milk. That was in the late forties."

To celebrate Center Market's fiftieth anniversary in 1987, Simmons published a copy of his first advertisement from September 10, 1937.

"I said, 'Of course we cannot sell what we did fifty years ago. No, we cannot sell at those prices, but to celebrate the event, we will sell on a first-come, first-serve basis twenty-five bushels of sweet potatoes at three pounds for ten cents and twenty-five bushels of fresh, local kale for a nickel a pound—four pounds for nineteen cents.'

"The farmer who served us all them years was Harry Bell from

Brookview. He was a nice farmer and he had first-class stuff. I told him: 'Harry, for next Friday I want twenty-five bushels of kale.' He used to give me about five for the weekend.

"He said, 'What?'

"I said, 'I want twenty-five bushels of kale.'

"He said, 'What are you gonna do with it?'

"'That's no trouble of yours,' I said. 'And then I want twenty-five bushels of sweet potatoes.'

"He said, 'Jim, you're kidding me.'

"I said, 'No.'

"He said, 'Have you told your son?'

"I said, 'I don't have to tell him.'

"So when it came out what I wanted to do, he said, 'Well, how are you gonna do it for a nickel a pound for kale? You can't sell it for that.'

"I said, 'I can if you sell it to me for the same you did twenty-five years ago, and that's what you're gonna do.' I said, 'You're gonna let me have twenty-five bushels of kale for the same price you charged me twenty-five years ago, and you're gonna charge me the same price for sweet potatoes.'

"He said, 'I can't do it.'

"I said, 'You better had.'"

"And did he?" I asked, after Simmons appeared to have concluded his story with the admonition to farmer Bell.

"Yep," he replied, and then abruptly said, "Look, I'm gonna have to go now, and you're story telling will have to wait."

Nora Foxwell, proprietor of Miss Nora's Store, died in her ninety-sixth year, still serving Elliott Island residents fourteen hours a day, seven days a week. She once told me with both humor and affection in her voice: "Old Jim is somethin'. When my husband, Lenny, was livin', he went down one day early in the spring, and Jim had string beans in baskets in front of the store with a sign on 'em that said: 'Elliott's Island string beans.'

"Now in times back we grew early stuff here and carried it up to Cambridge, but our string beans wasn't ready yet. So Len says,

'Jim,' he says, 'our string beans hadn't even blossomed down there yet.'

"Old Jim smiles and says, 'Keep your lip, Len.'

"I don't know where he got them string beans."

Beating the Odds
on the Nanticoke

While men of African descent were commonplace aboard ships during the seventeenth and eighteenth centuries—serving as whalers, fishermen, merchantmen, even as Chesapeake Bay pilots—rarely have they been mentioned in historical documents or named as a ship's owner or commander. The exception is found in "Memoirs of an African Captain," the detailed account of Paul Cuffe's 1796 voyage to the Nanticoke River, which was published in 1807 in London's *Monthly Repository of Theology and General Literature* and authenticated in "Brief Memoirs of the Life of Capt. Paul Cuffe" by the Delaware Society for Promoting the Abolition of Slavery.

Paul Cuffe (1759-1817) was one of ten children composing the family of former slave Saiz Slocum and his Wampanoag Indian wife. Born on Cuttyhunk Island and reared in Dartmouth and Westport, Massachusetts, Paul grew up proud of his African heritage and soon abandoned the surname of his father's former Quaker owner in favor of Cuffe, the Anglicized form of Kofi, his family's African name. In Ashanti, Kofi means "born on Friday."

Cuffe went to sea as a whaler at the age of fourteen, and afterwards, still in his teens, risked his life and freedom by running the British blockade between Dartmouth and Nantucket during the American Revolution, all the while diligently studying the sciences of mathematics and navigation.

Signing aboard a coastal trader to North Carolina as mate, the energetic youth returned as ship's master. Then, after a period of modest maritime ventures with his Native American brother-in-law, Michael Wainer, Cuffe underwrote construction of *Sunfish*, a twenty-five ton schooner, aboard which he whaled along the Grand Banks, taking six of the giant mammals in a single season and demonstrating his bravery and skill by personally harpooning his prey.

In the Quaker community of Westport, where Cuffe lived most of his life, the rights of African and Native Americans were publicly espoused; but while the town's citizenry accepted the industrious and successful minorities among them, members of these races faced clear social and political limits.

Although the government taxed them in the same manner as fully franchised citizens, laws prohibited blacks from voting—a circumstance that prompted Cuffe to file a suit against the state in 1780. It was through his efforts that blacks were granted the right to vote in Massachusetts in 1783.

Cuffe's Pequot Indian wife, Alice, and his sister, Mary Wainer, bore thirteen children between them, and the six Wainer boys eventually formed the core of the Cuffe-Wainer crews. Mary's name was given to a newly constructed, forty-ton schooner, aboard which the two merchants entered the New England coastal trade.

Then, in 1795, Cuffe decided to construct a still larger vessel. The *Ranger*, a sixty-nine-ton, square-rigged schooner would extend his trading to more distant places, but it would also require larger capital. To finance the new vessel, *Sunfish* and *Mary* were sold and a cargo valued at $2,000 was secured for *Ranger*.

Poor communications at the time made almost any trading venture a gamble. Cuffe had little information about commercial conditions in other parts of the country, but he believed that some of the southern states would furnish a market where he could trade for profit; and since his investment in *Ranger* represented nearly his total assets, success was essential. Cuffe eventually initiated a triangular trade between three continents and became the wealthiest man of color in America, but as he ventured into Chesapeake Bay in 1796, his future was anything but secured.

Docking first at Norfolk, Cuffe learned that an exceptionally large crop of Indian corn had been harvested that year on Maryland's Eastern Shore and that he could likely procure a schooner load for a low price at a town named Vienna. The captain turned to his charts and plotted a course across the bay, through Tangier Sound and into the wide mouth of the Nanticoke River.

At the turn of the nineteenth century this Chesapeake tributary was hardly a recommended venue for an African American. Still mostly wild and remote, the lowlands bordering the Nanticoke supported small plantations, poor by comparison to their more southerly contemporaries or even those in nearby Talbot County. The region's economy was sustained by slavery, and it was regulated by a citizenry that not only held little affection for blacks but also feared them.

Slavery had then prevailed on the Nanticoke for more than a century, and although they shared the racial heritage of Cuffe and his crew, the field hands and even the skilled workers who labored in servitude along the river had little in common with *Ranger's* freeborn sailors. They had never held a license to come and go as they pleased, nor to pursue their own economic independence, a standing that Cuffe and his men viewed as their natural rights.

The area's European population was primarily a mixture of growers and foresters. The latter, having little interest in property, had preferred to trade with the British during the Revolutionary War rather than fight for what they considered to be foolish principles, and some among them constituted a predatory element.

In a few years the Cannon-Johnson gang, using the Nanticoke as a base, would gain notoriety by kidnapping both free blacks and slaves in Maryland, Delaware and surrounding states and selling these hapless victims into slavery throughout the South.

Moreover, Congress had just instituted the Fugitive Slave Act, legalizing the seizure of any black persons, pending proof of their status; and the Maryland Legislature had, within the year, passed a law requiring free blacks suspected of illegal activity to serve six months of servitude.

Since a vessel owned and operated by African Americans was unheard of on the Eastern Shore in that age, Cuffe and his crew were certain to fall under suspicion and were clearly at risk unless they carried irrefutable documentation of their freedom and of the ownership of *Ranger* and its cargo.

Some dozen miles inland, where the river narrows and begins a series of sweeping bends, *Ranger* passed Weston, the plantation residence of John Henry. Educated at Princeton and schooled in the law at London's Inns of Court, Henry had served in the Continental Congress, as governor of Maryland and finally in the United States Senate. The grower remained angry over having lost his slave property in 1780, when they were lured away by British promises of freedom.

Cuffe's biographers inform us that with the sudden and unexpected appearance of *Ranger*, the citizens of Vienna were filled with astonishment and alarm. They viewed the outsiders as troublemakers, and their race automatically stigmatized the sailors.

One wrote: "A vessel owned and commanded by a person of color and manned with a crew of the same complexion was unprecedented and surprising. The white inhabitants were struck with apprehensions of the injurious effects which such circumstances would have on the minds of their slaves, but perhaps they were still more fearful that, under the veil of commerce, he [Cuffe] had arrived among them with hostile intentions." Slave owners "probably suspected a secret intention to kindle the spirit of rebellion and excite a destructive revolt among their slaves."

It was not an entirely unfounded paranoia that gripped Vienna's property holders. Three years earlier, Tussaint L'Ouverture had successfully overthrown the French in Haiti, thereby igniting fears that equally destabilizing black revolutionaries might be bound toward the southern states. In fear that imported slaves might hail from the rebellious West Indies, Maryland had halted all new importation.

Nor would Vienna residents have been comforted to know that the incoming crew shared Native American descent. Combative relations with the nearby Nanticoke Indians dated back to John Smith's 1606 voyage of exploration. The colonists had cast the Nanticokes as adversaries from the beginning, and continued animosity characterized relations between the natives and the Europeans to the end of the eighteenth century.

But the crop of Indian corn was there, awaiting the first outbound vessel whose captain could strike a deal.

Initially, fear of the dark-skinned ship's company barred success, and several persons formed an association to attempt to prevent Cuffe from entering his vessel or remaining among them.

The burden of decision fell upon the recently appointed collector of customs, James Frazier, only the second such federal official to serve in Vienna. Frazier apparently knew this business. He found Ranger's registry at Bedford and receipts from known, reliable merchant houses to be correct, and they precluded any legal denial of the schooner's entrance.

As a deal for the grain was struck and the cargo loaded, Cuffe and his crew were able to achieve a measure of acceptance in the doubting community. "Drawing upon his Quaker values," a biographer relates, "Paul combined prudence with resolution. Although his schooner was entered in opposition to the association, he did not assume an air of triumph, nor use the language of defiance to his opposers. He conducted himself with candor, modesty, and firmness, and all his crew behaved not only inoffensively, but with a conciliating propriety."

Within a few days the association apparently vanished and the inhabitants treated Cuffe and his crew with respect and even kindness. Vienna residents boarded the Ranger to inspect her and visit with the crew, and one of the town's citizens, reportedly, invited the captain to his home for dinner.

After three weeks in Vienna, Cuffe was ready to retrace his course down the Nanticoke River and Chesapeake Bay. Once past the Virginia Capes, he steered northeast for New Bedford, where his cargo brought a profit of $1000, a significant financial accomplishment for that day. Cuffe was now firmly on his way to becoming the wealthiest African American of his time and the largest employer of his race in the nation.

Cuffe returned to the Nanticoke with the same lucrative results and also entered his ship in the coastal trade between Passamaquoddy Bay in Maine and Delaware River ports. Philadelphia and Wilmington newspapers of the period reported landings of gypsum cargoes by *Ranger* to rejuvenate Middle Atlantic soils that had been depleted by years of poor agricultural practices.

In 1800, Cuffe built the hundred-and-sixty-ton *Hero*, which eventually made eight voyages around the Cape of Good Hope while establishing a trade between East Africa and Europe. His largest vessel was *Alpha*—two hundred and sixty-eight tons—which the trader sailed to Sweden from Savannah, Georgia, in 1806.

Meanwhile, in Massachusetts, Cuffe's maritime success made it possible for him to purchase nearly two hundred acres of real estate and construct a gristmill and windmill, business ventures which included partnerships with both Quakers and people of color.

Cuffe's prosperity also enabled him to pursue his dream of a community school for all children, regardless of race; but in that endeavor he quickly discovered his limits. Even in his relatively free-thinking Massachusetts community there was no room for such a degree of racial toleration, and efforts by Friends to establish their own Quaker school stalled Cuffe's petition.

"Perceiving that all efforts to procure a union of sentiment were fruitless," his Delaware memoir reported, "Paul set himself to work in earnest and had a suitable house built on his own ground."

Supported financially by Cuffe, the school operated for years afterward, but a visitor to Westport noted that it was "tauntingly called 'Cuff's School' by persons who gladly sent their children."

Despite the unprecedented extent of his personal success, Cuffe became convinced that a black man could never achieve true social acceptance in America, so when news of a British program to repatriate blacks to Sierra Leone was announced, he sailed first to England and then to Africa to investigate the project, carrying with him a letter of introduction from President Thomas Jefferson.

Cuffe hoped that he might assist in creating a strong African nation that could succeed in commerce with Great Britain and the

United States and dissuade a continuation of the slave trade.

The War of 1812 interrupted Cuffe's maritime ventures and emigration plans until 1815, when he transported thirty-eight free individuals of his race to Sierra Leone and secured homesteads for them. But failing health prevented further trips, and the man who had triumphed against overwhelming odds to become the wealthiest African American in the nation died on September 9, 1817. His remains lie at rest in the Quaker cemetery in Westport, Massachusetts.

The Only Known Image of Paul Cuffe

Zip Code 21869

L ike country stores, the small-town post office that requires residents to pick up their mail each day is rapidly becoming an anachronism. For many of us, that's not a bad thing; we'd rather not take time from our busy schedules to venture much beyond our front doors to collect the assortment of envelopes bulging with bills and the "junk" postings of questionable enterprises seeking our hard-earned dollars.

I'm different. Even though I can have my mail delivered to a receptacle only a short leg-stretch from my desk, I rent a post office box in a town several miles distant, where the USPS does not yet grant residents the luxury of home delivery. It isn't the daily drive to Zip Code 21869 that I relish; it's the lives that I encounter there. I look forward to the smiles and greetings, the news I learn and the stories I hear.

It was a visit to 21869 that gave me the idea for an article that later became the title for one of my books—*You Still Can't Get to Puckum.* Shortly after publication of what I refer to as Puckum 1, *You Can't Never Get to Puckum,* I bumped elbows with an octogenarian in the lobby one day.

"Have you ever found out how to get to Puckum yet?" he greeted me.

"Still looking," I shot back. "Why don't you get busy and find the answer for me."

"I don't think nobody understands about Puckum," the little man with a several-day growth of stubby, white whiskers remarked seriously. "You go on up there, and they say, 'Hey, you got to go up a little further.' And after you go up a little further, you got to go up a little further more, and in the end you still ain't never have found it. It's just gone. I imagine Puckum was gone when they started lookin' for it. You never could get to Puckum, and *you still can't get to Puckum.*"

Seemingly insignificant encounters such as that often have far reaching implications on my thinking and my work. Sometimes I rush back to my desk and begin to hammer the keyboard. More often, the thoughts and ideas need to ferment and be joined with others before they push me into action. Now and then I am fortunate enough to collect stories that are complete in their own right. Take the incident of the twenty dozen bullfrogs that was offered to me in the parking lot at 21869 recently.

"You're always askin' for a story," the man began. "You won't believe this, but it's the truth. My father was a big bullfrogger—a big coon hunter and big bullfrogger. I've got pictures of him back in 1910 with hides hangin' on the wall. I got so I went with him. We coon hunted a lot and we frogged a lot.

"They always say it's the tenth of May. You can bet on that!

"My father's brother was one of the first ones that they drawed on the draft [World War II], and he was one of the first ones that come home. He come home in '45, and right away he wanted to go bullfroggin'. He had never been with Daddy for a long time. Of course Daddy and him are both dead now.

"My uncle lived down toward Cambridge, down to Aries, and that's the Transquakin' River there. We put over right at the bridge this night. We had a little skiff and Daddy paddled. I set in the middle seat, holdin' the granner bag; so when you catch 'em, you put 'em in there.

"A granner bag is a hundred and sixty-seven pound bag of fertilize. I'm talkin' about a *real* granner bag now. It would hold ten

154

dozen, and then you had to tie it. But when you got ten dozen in it, that was a lot of frogs in there to be on the bottom, and that was all the weight you could carry.

"My uncle got up in front and started to catch 'em, goin' down the river. In the night that they lay [eggs]—that's the tenth of May— they go out in the river and you find a lot of 'em two at a time. They were just as tame; you just reach down and pick 'em up. After that night you couldn't get close to 'em with a crab net, but that night they just sit right there.

"So Richard was startin' to catch 'em and I was catchin' some. Daddy kept on paddlin'. I caught not ten dozen, but I had six more to go, and I never got 'em before we quit. Richard had ten dozen, so we had nineteen dozen and a half. I always called it twenty dozen, but if you want to be legal about it, it was nineteen dozen and six. That's a lot of frogs now, I want to tell you.

"Daddy would always send 'em to the railway depot in East New Market to two places in Baltimore that I can remember, in little cantaloupe crates. He'd send 'em live, like two dozen and a half in a crate—feet would stick out of there—to a place called J. W. Chews. And there was another place up there. It was Monumental Company, but now, what kind of a company it was, I don't know. It wasn't crab. Maybe it was seafood, but anyway, it was Monumental.

"So anyhow, we come home—that old Hawkeye house where I lived, down there to the branch. Up where we were, the water stays about six inches in that ditch, but it will come up in the woods a ways when you have a big rain.

"We went home and built this thing in the nighttime, and I'm talkin' about late, too. It must have been eleven, twelve o'clock. We were at least that late. We took long boards we were gonna put on that shed, but we never did build it and the boards rotted. Anyhow, it happened to be a time when we had them boards. We built this thing—just slats—about two boards high. We built it about fifteen feet by three or four feet and put it in the ditch, and we put the frogs in there. We put it so they could all get up on the bank.

"It come a storm that night, and this is the part I'm tellin' you about. This is what I've led up to. I mean catchin' twenty dozen frogs was somethin', too, but it all led up to this.

"I thought about it this year on that night—the night of May the tenth. I was sittin' around there, and I said to her, 'Well, you know what tonight is?' It's like on December the seventh some people will say, 'You know what today is?' That's Pearl Harbor Day. So I said, 'Do you know what tonight is?'

"She said, 'No.'

"I said, 'This is the night we caught twenty dozen bullfrogs.'

"Then I thought about you. I said, 'I'll tell him this when I see him, and he never will believe me.' When you tell the truth about somethin' like that, you know, it's hard to believe. It's like Ripley. A lot of times the real truth is so crazy that nobody will never believe it.

"Well, anyhow, it come up a big thunderstorm, just like we had here about two weeks ago. It was just a real slow bank there, and the water come slantin' up—went up in the woods—and them bullfrogs, they every one drownded.

"Now, you don't believe that, do you?"

Next to the post office is an empty lot. The house that stood there once belonged to a notorious town doctor who moved to 21869 shortly after the turn of the twentieth century. I learned about him in the lobby one day.

"Man, he was a character," an old gentleman offered. "He was a Spanish-American War doctor, and I think he was a captain. He came up here from some town on the other side of the river. They say he was so damned mean they chased him out of there.

"He delivered me, and he and I were buddies, but he was a hard man, I'll tell you that. And he wasn't foolin' either. He was just as rough as he said he was.

"When he leaned on me, I always came to his rescue. I didn't have a car, but my father had a car. Years back, there was something similar to taxis. For so much [fee] you could get what they called 'hired tags,' and they had a 'H' on the tag. Like you came up here on a boat and you wanted to go to Hurlock, you'd tie up and get someone with a hired tag to carry you on up there. So that's what the old doc used to do with me. He'd always let me know plenty ahead of time, and if he said two o'clock, he meant two o'clock, not one minute after or before.

"He was a noble lookin' man—a clean-cut man. He didn't go out of his house till he was shaved and had his hair slicked back. He was always immaculate. When he'd come out on the street, even if he went to the post office [which then was in a building across the street from its present location], he would be freshly shaved, his hair combed, and he'd have a white, stiff-collared shirt on. He always walked straight as an arrow, just proud, you know.

"His wife was a fine, intelligent woman, and she was a right good nurse. She helped him with his patients. When he was makin' his rounds and she needed him, she would hang a flag out as a signal for him to stop.

"Doc hated cats and dogs. He'd kill 'em. He didn't want 'em to come on his property. He had concrete drains instead of just a ditch like everybody else. He had his shrubbery trimmed and everything spotless. One time some kittens came in his yard and he called 'em over and cut their heads off with a hedge shears.

"Some folks used to have camp meetin's, and unless they killed somebody, it wasn't much of a meetin'. So somebody cut this boy one night, and they brought him in and set him in doc's waitin' room. He had a waitin' room in the front of the house, and he had all his medicines in another room. He had just scrubbed his floor that day, and when he opened the door and looked out there, he started to yell. 'Dammit,' he said, 'who bled on my floor?'

"A patient said, 'It's this man, doctor. He's cut bad.'

"'Well,' Doc said, 'I don't want no son-of-a-bitch bleedin' on my clean floor. Get him out of here.'

"And he ran him out of there. You'd be in big trouble now to run somebody out like that.

"He kept a old skullcap in his office. There was a bunch gamblin' one time, and they knocked a man in the head—killed him. He had a hole in the top of his skull where he got hit with a stick. Doc had to perform a autopsy on him, so he took a hacksaw and sawed the top of the man's skull off. He sawed all the way around that man's head and took the cap right off, and he had it in his office as

157

a souvenir. He never got in any trouble. Most people were afraid of him. I wouldn't want to cross his path.

"Then there was the man that owned the hotel in Baltimore. He had a heart attack while he was duck huntin' down on Fishin' Bay, but he had a accidental clause in his insurance policy for double indemnity. Doc had to examine him, and he pronounced him dead from drownin' so they'd get the double indemnity. I imagine Doc got a piece of it too. He was so damn crooked he could lay down on a corkscrew, but he was good to me.

"He was diabetic and finally had one of his legs removed. That put him out of commission. And then he lost his other leg, and you talk about cussin'. You could have sent that man to hell and it wouldn't be hardly as bad as cripplin' him up like that.

"He had plenty of money, so he went into a place up in Baltimore that had everything right there in one buildin'—assisted livin'. He's been gone a long time now.

And there are also tender moments at 21869.

I see her often, slowly measuring the four main thoroughfares of town with her cane, tarrying for long moments at the river, her hair as white as snow in the morning sun. This day we met at the heavy, plate glass door, and I held it open for her to enter. In one hand she clutched a slightly wilted bouquet of tickseed sunflowers, those wild, abundant, butter-yellow blooms that gladden the late August and September roadsides. When I admired them, she replied, "They remind me of a poem."

"Which one?" I asked with interest.

"I'll tell you the last verse of it. I won't tell you the rest because it goes on too long. I thought of it when I saw these," she said, lifting the blooms from her side.

"'For many a flower is born to blush unseen and waste its sweetness on the desert air.' And that's so true. Nobody sees them. They just go by themselves."

"I see them," I said. "I see them everywhere, and I've heard the poem. They're both lovely."

"If you know that poem, then you know the one about the river. It says, 'For men may come and men may go, but I go on forever.'

"I find myself quoting that when I stand down by the river. It's beautiful today. There's just enough sun that it's catching each of the little rivulets."

I told her that I once lived in Pennsylvania where the rivers do, indeed, go on forever. "But ours," I suggested, "comes and goes twice a day with the tides."

She laughed.

"It has been so nice talking with you today," I told her. "When I see you again, will you quote another poem for me?"

"I had a teacher who loved poetry so much," she replied. "A little girl—Miss Ranny. She was no bigger than a minute, and she had brown eyes. She didn't like the boys, but she liked the girls who liked poetry. I'm amazed how much I remember from my school days."

Should they ever decide to deliver the mail to Zip Code 21869, it will be a terrible loss to the practice of what little I possess in the way of social skills.

Graves of Richard Bennett III (left) and Wife, Elizabeth

Poor Dick o' Wye

When nationally acclaimed correspondent Dickson Preston went searching for the grave of Richard Bennett III in the summer of 1972, the Queen Anne's Historical Society was able to offer him only a vague idea of its location. With an 1886 *Baltimore American* article that described the site as lying in a patch of briars and weeds at the southern tip of Bennett's Point as his only guide, Preston headed down Bennett Point Road, inquiring along the way about old tombstones. "Like the man himself," Preston mused, "his grave seemed to have been curiously forgotten, almost as if a deliberate curtain of silence had been drawn."

As the road was about to terminate against the glistening waters of Wye River on Ice House Point, the discouraged journalist saw a young man washing a car in his yard and decided to make one final appeal. "I'm doing some historical research," Preston said. "Are there any old gravestones around here?"

"Yep," the lad replied. "Right over there behind the white fence."

"Mind if I take a look?"

"Help yourself."

The weathered boards confined a mother sow and her brood, but Preston's attention was attracted to a rectangular plot within the enclosure, completely overgrown by Virginia creeper, honey-

161

suckle, poison ivy and small trees. Amidst this greenery the corner of a stone marker lay exposed.

Putting the fence behind him, the now hopeful writer began to pry away the vines with a stick, soon revealing the name of Dorothy Carroll. That was a disappointment, for Preston knew of no Dorothy Carroll who might have been buried with Richard Bennett.

But there was another stone beneath the tangle of vines, and additional effort bared the name "Elizabeth." Preston's pulse quickened; Richard Bennett had been married to Elizabeth Rousby. He began to tear with his hands at the thick mat over yet another massive, granite vault cover and soon exposed a coat of arms. Beneath it were the chiseled words: "Here lieth the body of...." Preston gave another hard yank at the vegetation and the name "Richard Bennett, Esq." appeared.

The land that is currently referred to as Bennett's Point was patented to Henry Morgan by Cecil Calvert in 1658, in payment for Morgan's transportation of two indentured servants to the province. The grant was originally called Morgan's Neck. Then, around 1698, the three-hundred-acre property descended to Elizabeth Rousby, Morgan's granddaughter, who shortly afterward married Richard Bennett III.

Although he has been called one of the most remarkable men in Maryland history, the odds are heavy against your ever having heard of Richard Bennett III. He led no army, headed no government, wrote nothing to inspire the ages, but he was Delmarva's first multimillionaire and the wealthiest man in North America during the first half of the eighteenth century. Richard Bennett owned more land, more ships, more slaves, more livestock, and in a time when tobacco was king, he produced more of that "divine herb" than did any other man on the continent.

The first Richard Bennett was a Puritan governor of Virginia. He negotiated the "perpetual" treaty of 1652 with the Susquehannock Indians, and during the turbulent struggle between the English Roundheads and Cavaliers—a political war that culminated with Oliver Cromwell's order to behead King Charles I—Bennett served as Cromwell's hatchet man in Maryland and Virginia.

Richard Bennett III was born on September 16, 1667, four months after his father, Richard II, drowned in the Wye River while duck hunting. Two years later the lad's mother, the former Henrietta Maria Neale, married Philemon Lloyd, a member of one of the most prominent families on the Eastern Shore of Maryland, and became mistress of Wye House.

Because of the many descendants that have been named for her, Madam Lloyd has sometimes been called "the great ancestress of the Eastern Shore." A strong-willed woman of great beauty and character, Henrietta was the daughter of one of Lord Baltimore's chief lieutenants, and her mother is said to have been a lady-in-waiting to Queen Henrietta Maria, wife of the executed King Charles. A mourning ring given by the queen to Bennett's grandmother survives in the collection of the Historical Society of Maryland.

Although Philemon Lloyd was a staunch Protestant, Richard's mother stubbornly insisted that Richard and his sister be raised as Catholics. At a time when Catholicism was considered no less than treason against the government of England, Henrietta succeeded in defending her faith while continuing to maintain and build upon her status as a romantic figure.

So Richard Bennett III grew to manhood as the stepson of a strong-willed, politically prominent, Protestant stepfather and an equally strong-willed and adored Catholic mother. While his half brother, Edward Lloyd II, climbed the political ladder toward the eventual governorship of Maryland, Bennett knew that as a Roman Catholic he could never achieve a comparable political career, and so he turned to the pursuit of wealth instead.

Richard was thirty years old when Henrietta Maria died, and shortly thereafter his name begins to appear on land records throughout the Eastern Shore. It is recorded literally hundreds of times on the books of Kent, Queen Anne's, Talbot and Dorchester Counties as purchaser, mortgager and forecloser.

At the same time, Bennett began to construct the greatest business empire the American Colonies had ever known. He built his own fleet, becoming the principal ship owner on the Chesapeake. He engaged in widespread trade with England, the West

Indies and the other American colonies. He established his own wholesale stores, trading his imports for tobacco and various raw materials. While other wealthy colonists enjoyed a life of pleasure and leisure, Bennett pursued additional wealth with an almost neurotic passion.

Richard Bennett entered upon his quest at the perfect time. The price of tobacco, upon which the economy of the times depended, had plunged, and Maryland was in an economic depression. Many planters went bankrupt or were anxious to sell and move on. Bennett began his buying spree when nearly everyone wanted to sell. With an abundance of cash on hand, he was able to purchase property and loan money with property as collateral. If payments did not promptly follow, foreclosure did. In addition, he acquired considerable land at little or no cost when owners failed to pay their ground rent, an equivalent to taxes at the time.

Bennett pursued one of his most ruthless transactions against a man named William Sweatnam, son of Richard Sweatnam, who had raided Wye House in 1689 and confiscated guns and ammunition from Bennett's mother on the pretext that she might arm the Indians. Henrietta rebuffed the raiders by taking Sweatnam to court and successfully demanding an apology and return of her property.

It was during Bennett's assault on Sweatnam that he acquired Wye Mill and the Wye Oak. It is doubtful that Bennett ever noticed the oak tree, then perhaps a century and a half old. He certainly could never have imagined that three hundred years later the tree would be internationally famous and he would be all but forgotten.

Not always a model of decorum, Bennett once rode with the Protestant clergyman John Lillingston and ten others to York—then the Talbot County seat on Skipton Creek—to protest the current government of Maryland. After partaking of a few drinks (the court doubled as a tavern), Bennett and his party interrupted the proceedings and were bodily ejected; but when the justices ended their session, the dissenters rode their horses into the empty courtroom and then imprisoned some of their members in the pillory and stocks outside. The frolic concluded in a free-for-all fistfight, but on the following day the debauchery was renewed at a picnic, where the participants became too inebriated to stand, some apparently falling or being thrown into Skipton Creek.

Upon testimony offered by the tavern's owner, claiming damage to his property, the group was arrested and removed to St. Mary's City for trial, where at least some of them were found guilty. Good fortune was on their side, however, and they were promptly pardoned as a gesture of clemency, "on account of His Majesty's happy success and late victory against the French."

We think of Maryland as the colony that most championed religious freedom, but its legislators often discriminated against Roman Catholics and others. In 1707 the General Assembly voted to prohibit the offering of mass, and residents of the province were denied the right to vote in 1718 unless they took an oath declaring, among other things, that "I abhor, detest and abjure, as impious and heretical, that Damnable Doctrine and Position, that Princes may be excommunicated [or that any foreign] Prelate...hath or ought to have any...authority, Ecclesiastical or Spiritual, within the Kingdom of Great Britain or any of the Dominion thereto belonging."

Bennett boldly stood against such religious persecution by providing financial and moral support to his church, and, with Charles Carroll and other prominent Catholics, he began to look elsewhere for a place to live. Carroll went so far as to travel to Paris and apply for a grant of land in French America, but his request included most of what is now the state of Arkansas and was too excessive for the French to concede.

And so, in the fall of 1749, at the age of 82, Richard Bennett remained a resident of Maryland and lay on his deathbed at Morgan's Neck. In a state of advanced physical and some say mental deterioration, he ordered that his old will be destroyed and a new one prepared. It was a complicated instrument of sixteen pages and named some two hundred and seventy-five beneficiaries, with the bulk of his estate bequeathed to Edward Lloyd III, the outspoken anti-Papist son of his half brother, Edward II.

The battle for Bennett's wealth was joined immediately. Witnesses agreed that he had signed the will, but did he know and understand the contents of the document? In spite of some affidavits to the contrary, the will was certified and Lloyd was named as its executor.

Within five days of the decision, descendants of Bennett's sister Susanna filed a "petition of libel" against Lloyd. A year passed with no resolution, and Governor Ogle finally appointed a commission that, after hearing all the testimony, approved the will as written, and the largest exchange of property in Maryland history up to that time finally took place.

Why would Richard Bennett leave the greatest fortune on the continent to a man who abhorred the religious convictions he held so dear? The answer, Dickson Preston felt, may lie simply in the fact that Lloyd, like Bennett himself, was a tough and practical businessman. The two had been partners in a number of enterprises, while those who contested the will had never been close to Bennett, and four of the five were women, or, as Preston put it: "mere females."

While we have learned that Richard Bennett III was capable of ruthlessness, the obituary that appeared in the Wednesday, October 18, 1749, *Maryland Gazette* indicates that he was primarily a man of great compassion and generosity.

"On the Eleventh Instant Died, at his capitol seat on *Wye*-River in *Queen Anne's* County, Richard Bennett, Esq.; in the Eighty-third Year of his Age, generally lamented by all that knew him. As his great Fortune enabled him to do much good, so (happily for many) his Inclination was equal to his Ability, to relieve the Indigent and Destressed [sic], which he did very liberally, without regarding of what Party, Religion, or Country they were. As he was the greatest Trader in this Province, so great Numbers fell in his Debt, and a more merciful Creditor could not be, having never deprived the Widows or Orphans of his Debtors of a Support; and when what the Debtors left, was not sufficient for that Purpose, frequently supply'd the Deficiency. His long Experience and great Knowledge in Business, as well as his known Candor and Generosity, occasion'd many to apply to him for Advice and Assistance, and none were ever disappointed of what was in his Power, and several were by his Means, extricated out of great Difficulties. He was always solicitious

166

[sic] to prevent Differences among his Neighbours, and to reconcile such as he could not prevent. In short, nothing gave him so much Pleasure as doing humane and benevolent Actions; and it may be truly affirm't, that by his Death, the Poor and Needy have lost their greatest Friend and Benefactor."

His funeral was reported in the Wednesday, November 8 edition of the *Gazette*: "On Wednesday last was solemaized [sic] the Funeral of Richard Bennett, Esq.; of *Wye*-river, in a very handsome and decent Manner, by the Direction of his sole Executor, the Hon. Col. Edward Lloyd. Mr. *Bennett*, by his Will, has forgiven above one hundred and fifty of his poor Debtors and has made Provision for the Maintenance of many of his Overseers, and other Dependents; and settled a Sum of Money to be paid annually to the Poor of a Parish in *Virginia*; and done many other Acts of Charity and Munificence. He was supposed to be the Richest Man on the Continent; and as he died without issue, he has, after making many large and handsome Bequests to others, left the Bulk of his Estate to his Executor."

In the fall of 1966, members of the Archaeological Society of Delaware began an eight-year excavation on Morgan's Neck, eventually uncovering the sites of seven buildings, including the one in which Bennett lived. It is believed that the house was destroyed by fire about 1765. Its foundation measured twenty-two by eighty feet, and the building probably contained two H-shaped chimneys. The recovered artifacts are deposited with the Maryland Archaeological Conservation Laboratory and consist of glass, ceramic, iron and lead objects and fragments.

Since the discovery of Bennett's grave and homestead, the peninsula has been developed into expensive waterfront estates. Jeremiah Banning, a prominent Talbot County sea captain, Revolutionary commander and statesman, and himself no stranger to the lifestyles of the rich and famous, once referred satirically to Bennett as "Poor Dick o' Wye." By today's standard of living on Bennett Point, its residents might well consider the peninsula's namesake to have been poor, for I am sure he had far less than they possess in the way of conveniences.

About A Ghost

This is another of the interviews I conducted with a group of elderly African Americans. The conversation opened with the question: "Have any of you ever seen a ghost?"

"**A**bout a ghost—you couldn't git me outside the door after dark. No indeed! I'se afraid he try to grab me. I never didn't see no ghost or no ghost light—only light bug is all I seen—but I was scared I *would* see one. I be goin' to work, walkin' out that big lane down there to Crapo, and I'd be scared to death. It was a long time for I come to myself—got used to it. People still be talkin' 'bout it, but everything wasn't so.

"We have a flood one time. The water raised up, and I seen a casket come up out the ground. It was floatin' on the water and nobody didn't know who it was. It went along with the tide and it went on down—on through the woods, just like a person would. And then, after a while it went away, and nobody don't know where it was at. I got scared. I was scared to go out there. I was afraid of the devil—the devil try to get me."

"I seen my mother after she died. I was layin' in bed. My little boy was havin' convulsions and I was sick myself. I have my other children in a room away from me, and I hear they say, 'I know who you is.'

"I say, 'I wonder what's the matter with my children.' I was sleepin' in the front room, and when I looked up, my mother lookin' down on me just like that. That's the truth; I'm tellin' you the truth. She lookin' down on me just like that [holds her hand to her forehead as though shielding her eyes from the light].

"I said, 'Oh Lord, Oscar,'—that's my husband's name. I said, 'Oh Lord, Oscar, there's Momma.'

"He said, 'Where?'

"I said, 'Standin' right over top of me.' I had pulled the cover over my face. I said, 'Oh Lord, Oscar, there's Momma; there's Momma!'

"Oscar says, 'Where your momma at? You know your momma dead.'

"And all at once I hear my stair steps: 'crack-up, crack-up.' They crack real loud.

"And I seen my father. My father never allowed us to go out and stay but so long. One time I and my sister went where Santa Clause was for small children, you know. We were the biggest and the oldest of the sisters, and my father, he was dead then.

"After we got along aways, my father walked out from there with a white shirt on and blue coat. I know just what he had on—white shirt, blue coat and black necktie—and he followed us home. He followed us home! My sister had left me and I was tryin' to catch up with her. My hair got tight on my head. My body got tight. I was tryin' to get away from him and he was walkin' right alongside of me, pattin' me on the shoulder.

"I'm tellin' you the truth. He followed me clear home to the house, and when he followed me clear home to the house, I rapped on the door. 'Momma, open the door! Open the door quick, Momma! Open the door!'

"Momma open[ed] the door and my hair got just as tight on my head. I said, 'Poppa's followed me home.' And it was him. I was about thirteen then. He didn't allow us to go out like that nowhere, so he followed us clear home.

"My sister didn't see him. I said, 'Didn't you see that man followin' us, Lisa?'

"She said, 'No, I didn't see no man.'

"I said, 'He followed us clear to the door.' My jaws got tight. My mouth got so tight. I'm tellin' you the truth."

"Yeah, that's the way. He didn't allow you to stay out but a certain length of time. My brother—I believe he was born to see—he told me one day: 'Sister, move out the way [of] all them spirits.'

"I said, 'Where then?'

"He said, 'I see 'em. I told you to move so they could get by you.'

"I was lookin' around, tryin' to find where they are. I ain't never seen 'em, but he did. It's like you see 'em and they vanish right on away from you."

"Yeah, that's what they do; they vanish right away. Mom say she saw her brother, and he was dead in Johns Hopkins Hospital."

"My brother saw the spirits all the time. He went down there to Crapo, some place where people used to get killed. He said he seen a-plenty of 'em. He went down there and stayed one night in the woods. I say, 'Why you stay in the woods? You see all these spirits. Ain't you afraid they gonna come and get you?'

"He said, 'No, I been used to seein' 'em.'

"And I'll tell you another thing. Do you remember that old house, like you goin' over there to the crab house? Well, my brother saw a man with no head on top that buildin'—say the man was up there on top the house with his suit on and no head. And he told me: 'There's some money in there.'

"And don't you know, two weeks after when he told me about it, these two, three little colored children and white children played together. Both didn't neither one had no money, and they went in that old house and found the money. Seems like it was cash money what they got.

"They went in the store uptown, and the woman ask them where did they get the money. Don't you know, honey, she took the money that they had and told the polices, and them polices went down there and helped theirselves with the money. They promise both them dear little white children and colored children that they was gonna get some, and they never did get none. All they got for it was a radio. I believe the polices divide it up with that store lady some way, and I know them dear little children need that money. That was a good while ago."

"I believe in ghosts 'cause I seen 'em. Lord have mercy, I seen 'em. I know dead people come back. I seen my mother come back. I was layin' in bed and it was dark. I wake up [and] somethin' tappin' up the steps: 'tap, tap, tap, tap,' just like it was a chicken pick at some feed. It come right through the door to where I was layin', and it was my mother came in. She wearin' a white dress—long—and she hold it up in her hand so it don't brush the floor. If I'm tellin' you a lie, I hope Jesus makes me fall right out a corpse."

"When my father was livin', we both worked, and every mornin' he'd get up and cook breakfast. But on a Sunday I had to cook breakfast then. And when my father died, the next Sunday mornin' somethin' shook me in the bed and woke me up, like he did when he was livin', for me to get up and cook breakfast."

"I knowed this woman give a birth, and she died the day after she give the birth. And don't you know, she come back for that baby. Her husband seen her in the room at night, and he try to grab her, but ever' time he try to grab her, she be someplace else. And next day, don't you know, that baby died. She come back for that baby—wasn't no other reason."

"When we was small, we'd sit and listen at 'em tell the ghost stories. They say it was an old lady—I can't remember her name— that they buried some money. Some people buried some money, and they cut her head off and buried her with the money. And we would sit and listen at 'em tell that story."

"That was Big Liz that they cut her head off, and they put her with the gold—down there in the Green Briar Swamp it was. Some man bury that gold in slavery times, and he have Big Liz help him. When they have anybody help him, then he kills that person and buries him with the gold so he won't tell. That's what he done with Big Liz, and that makes the gold hanted. Big Liz what you call a hant, uh huh. That's what she be. She hang around and watch out for that treasure. Before you ever find that, you gotta get over her."

"Oh, Lord, have mercy, that's all they would talk about. We used

171

to live down by Green Briar Swamp, and I got so I skeered go in the dark. I was skeered go to bed when it got good dark. Had some of the biggest mess I ever heard goin' on. Oh, Lord, help me so much."

"My father used to tell that one night him and his brother was walkin' along the road. He had a pistol and his brother told him, 'Boy, Big Liz gonna git after you and make you run and leave that gun.' He was walkin' along, and all at once somethin' fell right across the road ahead of him—like a ball and chain.

"His brother said, 'Hey, boy, where you at?'

"My father reached up and got his hat and he said, 'I don't know where you is, but I know I'm gone.'"

"One time down here to the Choptank, this man come to Uncle George and said he knew where some money was buried at. It was right next to the water. So they went there, and this man was a-diggin' and a-diggin'. He told Uncle George: 'George,' he said, 'when I get near it, don't say a word. You might see a bull, cow, anything come, but don't say nothin'.'

"So the man kept a-diggin' and a-diggin', and he struck a box. 'Uh oh, got it!' All of a sudden, Uncle George said, a bull come—snot runnin' out his nose, light on his head. Said he tried to never paid no mind, but the more the man dug, all kind of animals come right in his face, like they gonna run right over top of him—eyes flashin', snot runnin' out his nose, smoke comin' out his nostrils and ears.

"You're suppos' pay no mind and keep right on diggin', but Uncle George was scare. Finally, he couldn't stand it no more. He said, 'Damn, look at 'em comin'. Damn if I ain't goin' away from here.' And the money went right on down. That box where that money was in, it went further down. You can't say somethin' or the money go further down.

"Uncle George run—left the man—and they gone without gettin' the money. Man didn't count with Uncle George no more. You're suppose' go by yourself when you tryin' to find some money."

"Lots of people been tryin' to dig up treasure, and the ghostes wouldn't let 'em."

"Yeah, I heard about that too, but it was a man over there

toward Trappe way, he was lucky enough to get the money. You know that place goin' through there. It's an old church—just a frame like—and he heard people say there was money there. One night he went in the dark and started diggin'. He said he had a dime, so when the things started comin' up, he throwed that dime in there and kept right on. That's why he hit the pot. He seen horses kickin' and ever'thing else, but he stayed by it till he got that money. The next day he went and carried it to the bank. He bought two farms and had money enough to keep on with it. He was just the lucky one to get it."

"Sam went to bed one night and said somethin' come and shake him and woke him up. A man was at the foot his bed and kept pointin' and pointin' and pointin'. He told him where his money was at—down by the woods. Said, 'Don't tell nobody 'bout it.'

"First word come out Sam's mouth, he told his wife 'bout it. 'I'm goin' get that money.' But when he went there, it was a great big hole where the money was at, but it was gone. He said it really was true, but he shouldn't said nothin'."

"My husband's grandfather lived up to Church Creek. He said he was out one night long ago and comin' through the back road, and this ghost walk up to him. He started runnin', and he said the ghost started runnin' right along with him; and it said, 'I can run as fast as you can.' He said he run all the way home."

"I've really seen somethin' myself. My youngest son is passed about four years, and one night I was layin' on the lawn chair sleepin', and I woke up. He was standin' right close to me—just close to me as you are—and he turned and looked right at me. But he didn't stay long; it was like a flash of lightnin'. Somebody said that the spirit never dies.

"And then one night the current went off, and it was dark in the room. When I woke up, it was somethin' standin' by me, and it was gone just that quick. My other son was settin' there sleepin', and he doesn't know it today because I didn't tell him.

"And another time I was home by myself, and I woke up and it was like a shadow went behind the wood stove. I believe that was my husband. He passed in '82. I just believe that was him.

"And then another time when I was down to my son's house and I was hangin' out clothes, there was a wind goin', and somethin' brushed right by me and disappeared. My son hadn't passed no longer than about two months, and I just figured it was him. I looked, but I didn't see it no more, and it was a sunny day."

"A long time ago I and this man was walkin'. He had a girlfriend before, and somebody had drown her—throwed her in the lye pit down at Henson. They worked on sweet potatoes and had this lye for to take the skin off. That stuff'll burn the skin right off you. They called this guy 'honey dipper,' and he was likin' this woman. Somebody said he throwed her in this lye pit, only they couldn't prove it. He said she run in there.

"So I was walkin' along and this man was with me, and hot steam come out between of us. We got along by the house where she used be stayin' at—that house s'pose be hanted anyway—and that's when it come between of us. He had ahold of my arm, walkin' along, and all of a sudden it got so hot. I said, 'You feel that?'

"He said, 'Yeah.'

"Both of us felt the hot steam, but when we said somethin', it just went on its way. I said it was her—she didn't like me nowhere—but I don't know if it was her or not."

"There's a woman at night walks so far down that road at East New Market, and then she disappears. You go a certain time of night and you can see her. She used to watch this man's sheep at nighttime, and somebody killed her. It was a long time ago."

"We have this little branch near where I used live, and every time we would come through there—where it was little trees and things—the horse would rear up and start goin' fast. My father said the horse would see a ghost. It would do that ever' time we come through that branch. We would all look around. We didn't see nothin', but the horse would see the ghost."

"That's right. I hear a lot of people talk about a horse could see the ghost before anybody else could see it. All kinds of things happen way back then. If you went around the old folks, you could learn more about that stuff."

The
Ill-fated Chesapeake

Off Boston, Massachusetts, on Tuesday, June 1, 1813, the United States Ship *Chesapeake* engaged His Majesty's Ship *Shannon* in naval combat, an encounter that began at 5:50 p.m. with a salvo from *Shannon* and ended in hand-to-hand combat at 6:05 p.m. It was not America's finest fifteen minutes.

Six new frigates had been authorized in 1794 for use against the Barbary States of North Africa, but after a limited peace was achieved the following year, Congress canceled three of them, including *Chesapeake*.

Britain's perennial rival, France, then began to use the Jay Treaty between England and the United States as an excuse to seize American merchantmen, and interest in the vessels was renewed. Under orders of Secretary of the Navy Benjamin Stoddert, *Chesapeake's* keel was finally laid in the Virginia State Shipyard at Gosport on December 10, 1798, and the new man-of-war was prepared for launching in two hundred and sixty-five working days.

Chesapeake had problems from the start. As reported in the December 3, 1799, edition of the *Norfolk Herald*, the tallow on her ways froze in extremely cold weather and the forty-gun frigate refused to budge when her support blocks were pulled. One workman perished in the attempt to launch her. With considerable prodding, she finally made it to water on the following day.

Chesapeake departed from Hampton Roads on May 24, 1800, for her first wartime cruise and returned in early March 1801, after a treaty ending hostilities with France had been signed. In nearly a year of patrol along the southeastern coast of the United States and the West Indies, only a single prize had been taken, and there had been a minor rebellion among crew members over extended enlistments. Naval officials placed the frigate "in ordinary" at Gosport. Today we call it mothballing.

When the Barbary State of Tripoli declared war on the United States two months later, *Chesapeake* was hastily re-commissioned and dispatched to the Mediterranean in April 1802.

Four days out of Hampton Roads her mainmast broke, and the Atlantic crossing was completed under jury rig. In the following ten months she showed for only five days off the coast of Tripoli, spending the remaining time at Gibraltar, Leghorn or Malta, and then returned to Virginia and inactivity early in 1803.

An interesting journal entry was made on April 2, 1803, by Midshipman Henry Wadsworth, a member of *Chesapeake's* crew: "On the 22d Febry, it being the day after we left Algiers, Mrs. Low bore a son in the Boatswain's Store Room. On the 31st inst. (March) the babe was baptiz'd in the Midshipmen's apartment. The Contriver of this business was Melancthon Taylor Woolsey, a Mid who stood Godfather on the occasion & provided a handsome collation of Wine & Fruit. Mrs. Low being unwell, Mrs. Hays, the Gunner's Lady, officiated. Divine Service by Rev. Alex McFarland. The child's name— Melancthon Woolsey Low. All was conducted with true décorum & decency, no doubt to the great satisfaction of the parents, as Mr. Woolsey's attention to them must in some measure have ameliorated the unhappy situation of the Lady who was so unfortunate to conceive & bare [sic] on the Salt Sea. The other Ladies of the Bayviz: Mrs. Watson, the Boatswain's Wife, Mrs. Myres, the Carpenter's Lady, with Mrs. Crosby, the Corporal's Lady, got drunk in their own Quarters out of pure spite, not being invited to celebrate the Christening of Melancthon Woolsey Low."

Carrying women at sea on board ships-of-war was forbidden by a navy regulation of 1802, but the Mediterranean Squadron was plagued at that time with the problem of American sailors marrying native women, and that may explain the entry. No list of passengers has been found for this voyage home, although indications are that *Chesapeake* carried eighty-eight individuals in excess of the normal number aboard.

When Maryland-born William Ware and John Strachen, seamen aboard H. M. S. *Melampus*, deserted from the Royal Navy in 1807, England and France were still in conflict. Two damaged French ships had entered Chesapeake Bay in September 1806, laying up at Annapolis, and *Melampus* was part of a blockading fleet of British ships lying near the Virginia Capes.

Although Ware and Strachen had volunteered for duty in the Royal Navy and had accepted the payment of a bounty for their enlistment, American authorities believed they were United States citizens who had been pressed into British service. After British demands for their return were refused, Ware and Strachen exchanged their Royal Navy uniforms for American blue and were assigned to the frigate *Chesapeake*, prompting Vice Admiral George Cranfield Berkeley, Commander in chief of His Majesty's Fleet in North American waters, to issue an order to his captains to search the man-of-war for deserters, should she be encountered in neutral waters.

Early on the morning of June 22, 1807, *Chesapeake* weighed anchor at Hampton Roads and set sail again for the Mediterranean. As she passed through the capes, H. M. S. *Leopard* closed, and her commander demanded to board and search for deserters. Captain James Barron refused, denying there were any British deserters aboard. After firing a warning shot across *Chesapeake's* bow and receiving no concession from Barron, *Leopard* raked the American frigate with several broadsides, killing three of her crew and wounding eighteen others, including the captain. Completely unprepared for action, *Chesapeake* ineffectively returned fire with a single gun, lit by a live coal brought from below decks. A boarding party removed four seamen, including Ware and Strachen, and the wounded vessel limped back to port. Barron was later found guilty of negligence and suspended from command.

While the punishment for deserting the Royal Navy was commonly death, Ware and Strachen were sentenced—in consideration of their former good conduct—to receive five hundred lashes on their bare backs with a cat of nine tails. Mercifully, they were pardoned by the British commander in chief before the penalty was carried out.

The *Chesapeake-Leopard* affair is an incident taught in nearly all courses of American History, but unless you read *The Black Phalanx* by Joseph T. Wilson, you are not likely to know that Ware and Strachen were African Americans.

The encounter between U. S. S. *Chesapeake* and H. M. S. *Leopard* was an early incident in the chain of events which led to renewed hostilities between Britain and the United States, which climaxed in the War of 1812.

When Congress passed the Embargo Act, prohibiting American merchant vessels from sailing to foreign ports, *Chesapeake* was assigned to coastal patrol, for a time under the leadership of one of Delmarva's favorite sons—Captain Steven Decatur.

Meanwhile, British Captain Philip Bowles Vere Broke had been appointed to command His Majesty's Ship *Shannon* in June 1806 and was active in European waters for the next several years, keeping watch on Greenland whalers, participating in the capture of Madeira, serving with the Channel fleet and escorting a large convoy to the Mediterranean. While on duty in Lisbon, Broke received orders to proceed to Halifax, Nova Scotia.

Because of new regulations that forbade more than the most basic firing practice, gunnery in the Royal Navy had been in decline when Broke took command of *Shannon.* Understanding that quality arms and training were all important to readiness, the new captain fitted his guns with sights and elevation scales and marked the decks in degrees to assist his gunners. He ordered an hour and a half to be spent each day drilling with the great deck guns and another hour and a half at musketry, cutlass and boarding drill. Twice a week he directed target practice, paying for the extra shot and powder and for gunners' prizes out of his own pocket. When ordered from Lisbon to Halifax in 1811, Broke carried with him the best-trained crew in the Royal Navy.

On December 15, 1812, *Chesapeake* sailed from Boston Harbor to engage British shipping in the Atlantic, and while she was at sea, in late March 1813, H. M. S. *Shannon* was directed to maintain a watch on several American men-of-war being repaired in that New England port.

After four months at sea, *Chesapeake* returned to Boston, slipping past *Shannon* and another British frigate in a heavy fog on April 18.

On May 20, *Chesapeake* welcomed aboard a somewhat reluctant new commander. Having won a resounding victory over H. M. S. *Peacock*, Master Commandant James Lawrence had been promoted to the rank of captain, awarded the Congressional Medal and appointed skipper of the U. S. S. *Constitution* on May 4; but Secretary of the Navy Jones had a change of heart and reversed his order, assigning Lawrence to *Chesapeake* instead.

Lawrence inherited a crew that was angry at its previous captain and dissatisfied over pay and prize money due them. It included thirty British subjects, some of whom were deserters from the Royal Navy, as well as a number of disgruntled Portuguese. The lieutenant was ill on shore and the other officers were young and inexperienced.

As Lawrence prepared his ship to return to sea, Broke watched from just outside Boston Harbor. Knowing that he would soon have to return to Halifax, the British captain was spoiling for a fight.

In size and armament there was very little difference between the frigates. *Chesapeake* was slightly bigger and had a larger crew, but nearly a third were recent, inexperienced replacements.

The night of May 31 was squally, but June 1 dawned on a perfect summer day. Broke took *Shannon* in towards Boston Harbor, where he could see *Chesapeake* lying at anchor. He then went to his cabin and wrote a letter to Captain Lawrence that began: "Sir, As the *Chesapeake* appears now ready for sea, I request you will do me the favor to meet the *Shannon* with her, ship to ship, to try the fortune of our respective flags." In a spirit of exceptional chivalry, Broke went on to define in detail his armaments and manpower and offer assurances that no other ships of the Royal Navy would interfere in the proposed duel. A nearby fishing vessel was hailed and Broke placed an American prisoner aboard to deliver his letter to Lawrence.

Lawrence never received the written challenge. Broke's mere presence off Boston Harbor served as sufficient inducement for him to act.

At 12:30 p.m., Broke observed a flash and smoke as *Chesapeake* fired a gun and got under way, accompanied by a contingent of smaller boats carrying observers. Ashore, every place that provided a view of the two ships was crowded with people.

At 1:00 p.m., under full sail, *Chesapeake* passed Boston Lighthouse before a gentle westerly breeze and set a course to intercept *Shannon*, an action that would consume nearly five hours.

Finally, at 5:50 p.m., with only fifty yards separating the ships, *Shannon's* starboard battery opened fire and cannonading became general from both ships. In spite of the light breeze and the length of the approach, *Chesapeake* had closed with too much speed. To prevent his ship from drawing ahead of Shannon, Lawrence steered into the wind.

At 5:58 p.m., a cask of musket cartridges exploded on *Chesapeake's* quarterdeck, apparently ignited by a hand grenade thrown by Broke, himself. As the now badly wounded American frigate continued to turn into the wind, she lost her way and collided with *Shannon.*

Ordering his men to lash the ships together, Broke, sword in hand, leaped onto *Chesapeake's* quarterdeck with the cry: "Follow me who can!"

Lawrence fell, mortally wounded by a musket ball, and as he was carried below, he instructed an officer: "Tell the men to fire faster and not to give up the ship. Fight her till she sinks."

The battle was swift and deadly. By 5:05 p. m., fifteen minutes after the first shot had been fired, *Chesapeake's* crew was overcome. Lawrence's last command was "Burn her," but it was too late for further action.

Broke, although felled in the last few minutes of the battle by a

Hand-to-hand Combat aboard the Chesapeake

saber cut that exposed his brain, survived the action, but he never served at sea again. Lawrence died of his wounds four days later, in route to Halifax.

A few months afterward, several women stitched the words "Don't give up the ship" onto a flag and presented it to Oliver Hazard Perry, then commander of the U. S. S. *Lawrence*, which had been named in honor of Captain James Lawrence. On September 13, 1813, flying the flag in the battle of Lake Erie, Perry captured an entire squadron of British vessels, and "Don't give up the ship" became the motto of the United States Navy.

The U. S. S. *Chesapeake* was led triumphantly into Halifax Harbor, repaired, and removed to England where she served in the Royal Navy until placed in ordinary in 1816.

Sold to an individual named Holmes for five hundred British pounds in 1820, she was dismantled for building materials to construct several houses in Portsmouth, England, and timbers from her gun deck were used to construct Chesapeake Mill, which still stands at Wickham in Hampshire.

On June 30, 1899, a Naval Academy training ship was christened *Chesapeake*, but, wary of the ignominious reputation of her namesake, Captain Seaton Schroeder, Director of Naval Intelligence, petitioned the Secretary of the Navy in 1905 to change her name, and the second *Chesapeake* became *Severn.* No American warship since has carried the name of the nation's greatest estuary.

Above: Captains Broke (left) and Lawrence

Below: The Shannon and Chesapeake Engaged

183

The Death
of a Chesapeaker

" **A** fter several years of researching the migration of families
from the Eastern Shore of Maryland in the middle third
of the nineteenth century," remarked Sharon Moore, "Pat
Pigg and I began to refer to Northeast Texas as 'Chesapeake West.'"

Texans Moore and Pigg have been absorbed in genealogical research for a combined total of nearly four decades and have discovered some startling ties to Delmarva. Many family traditions and
histories in the Lone Star State contain tales of forebears who came
from the East with the "Chesapeakers."

A variety of reasons prompted emigrants to forsake their comparatively safe and bountiful homeland in the Mid-Atlantic for an
undeveloped and inhospitable frontier. Texas offered a fresh start
with new and exciting opportunities. Land could be had for the
asking—or for the taking—and no law pursued a man who was
wanted by authorities back home. In 1836 in that newly independent republic, an individual's physical strength, audacity and supply of gunpowder frequently determined the outcome of business
transactions and disputes as well, and there was an appalling a-
mount of violence. Annexation by the United States in 1845 brought
little immediate change to that turbulent border country.

Rabbit Creek, an insignificant tributary of the Sabine River, rises in Smith County, near Douglas, a community not large enough to be included on the Official Texas Travel Map. For twenty miles the rivulet meanders toward the northeast, passing Kilgore, home of the famed, high kicking Kilgore Rangerettes and the geographic center, in the 1930s, of the greatest concentration of oil derricks in the world.

East Texans call this region the "Piney Woods." It is a terrain characterized by low, rolling hills, cloaked in stands of pine and a wide variety of hardwoods. Low bushes of sumac edge the forest, and here and there a prickly Spanish dagger attracts the eye. Everywhere, the underbrush is dense.

Kilgore librarian Edgar Rachall lived his first twenty-five years within three hundred yards of Rabbit Creek. "Up until the 1950s," he told me, "it had quite a bit of water."

Rachall describes the width of the streambed as being from ten to fifty feet across from bank to bank. "That's not the water, now," he cautions. In dry seasons the depth will range from ankle-deep in the shallows to shoulder-deep in the larger pools. Dams have reduced the flow of most of the region's waterways.

"When I was a child," Rachall recalled, "I found arrowheads all the time. There were a lot of Indians living along Rabbit Creek in the 1800s. The Caddo were the predominant tribe."

Sometime between July 1852 and January 1853, Jinette Page, in company with her son, Eligah, and her son-in-law, Josephus Moore, left Leon County with a small herd of cattle and horses on a hundred-and-fifty-mile drive to Harrison County.

Jinette's husband, David Page, an accused murderer, had been lynched without trial by a lawless mob in 1840, and her daughter Mary Jane, Moore's wife, had died earlier in 1852. The drivers' destination may have been Marshall, where Josephus' brother was in the horse-trading business, or perhaps Jinette was moving cattle to better range on property she owned west of Marshall. About thirty miles from the end of their journey, near to where the town of Kilgore would be founded twenty years later, the small party stopped along Rabbit Creek and confined the stock in a makeshift corral.

Whether the Indian attack came as a surprise to the campers or was the result of some action on their part can only be surmised. Eligah was shot through the cheek by an arrow but managed to escape with his mother. Josephus Moore was killed.

Sixteen days after the incident, when Eligah had recovered enough to travel, Jinette Page and her son returned to Rabbit Creek. The cattle were found alive, still confined by the corral, but the horses were missing. Jinette and her son buried the remains of Josephus in a shallow, unmarked grave on the sandy banks of the winding waterway.

Pat Applewhite, one of twenty-five hundred remaining Caddo in East Texas, can see Rabbit Creek from her office window in City Hall. "It's just a little-biddy creek," she offered, "but everybody in Kilgore knows it. "I'm going to cruise down to Rabbit Creek," she mimicked what is apparently a common town proclamation.

Applewhite confirmed what I had already learned—that the nineteenth-century Caddo were a peaceful agricultural people who lived in stable villages and were not inclined to raiding. "We didn't have a lot of excitement in our lives," she said. Then she added: "Of course your people might have done something to incite them to attack. Then the Caddo could have done it."

Literally hundreds of tribes or clans of Native Americans were present in Texas in the 1850s, and nearly a dozen lived or hunted in the Kilgore area. Under the control of Mexico, Texas had become the horse-and-gun frontier for the Western Indian and a buffer between competing European powers, French and English traders introduced the firearm and Spain contributed the mounts.

The acquisition of the horse, especially, produced nothing less than a cultural, technological and economic revolution among the natives, enabling bands to freely move about, intensify their trading and raiding activity and hunt more effectively. Outsiders such as the Apache, Kiowa and Comanche migrated into the southern plains to be near the supply of horses.

The Comanche operated in loosely connected and far-ranging bands that fluctuated in size with the popularity of the leaders, and war honors and the number of horses taken from enemies determined rank and social status within their tribe. Horses were the measure of one's worth, and horse raiding and trading characterized the Comanche role in Texas. We will never know with certainty who killed Jinette Page's son-in-law, but if his bones should ever be discovered, my wager is that Comanche arrow points will be lying among them.

When Josephus Moore died on the banks of Rabbit Creek in the autumn of 1852, he was a long way from the land of his birth, and this devious man took with him a great secret—a guarded past that would remain hidden from Texans and from his own descendants for nearly a century and a half.

Moore was born on Delmarva, possibly in Eastville, Virginia, perhaps in Dorchester County, Maryland, and probably in 1795. Shortly afterwards, his family moved to an eighty-acre holding called "Blunderbush" on Broad Creek in Sussex County, Delaware, just upstream and within sight of its mouth on the Nanticoke River. Today, the property is owned by the state and known as Phillips Landing, a popular park and boat ramp.

As a young man, Moore became involved in the kidnapping of free African Americans and soon achieved notoriety matched by few others of his time. From Philadelphia to Baltimore and across the Delmarva Peninsula, his raids spanned several states, and his hapless victims were sold into slavery from the District of Columbia down the Atlantic Coast and across the South as far as Louisiana.

He was a principal figure in one of the most ruthless criminal gangs in the history of the nation. A reward was offered for his arrest in Pennsylvania, and Delaware leveled indictments against him on multiple charges of murder; but by fleeing south with his family and fortune, Moore successfully evaded authorities and was never apprehended. Josephus Moore was, in reality, Joe Johnson—Joseph Moore Johnson—the son of Captain Ebenezer Johnson, the "Pirate of Broad Creek," and the former son-in-law of Patty Cannon, "the wickedest woman ever to walk on American soil."

The Flight
of Joe Johnson

On March 1, 1826, for the sum of $1,000, Joe and Ebenezer Johnson transferred the deed to a home at Johnson's (or Wilson's) Cross Roads to Patty Cannon. This transaction provides the last documented evidence of the brother's presence on Delmarva and signals an end to the long and brutal reign of the Cannon-Johnson gang.

Joe had acquired the crossroads property from James Wilson on July 14, 1821, the same day on which a writ to recover three kidnapped victims was issued against him by the State of Delaware. While there is no mention of improvements in the contract between Wilson and Johnson and mystery surrounds both the construction and the fate of the original lodging there, we can say with certainty that the much-remodeled dwelling in Reliance, Maryland, proclaimed by a state historical marker to be "Patty Cannon's House" and now often referred to as "Joe Johnson's Tavern," is not the building into which Patty moved in 1826.

Patty's husband, Jesse Cannon, had died a few years earlier, apparently in 1822, and by 1825 the gang's activities had attracted the attention of authorities from Pennsylvania to Mississippi. With a noose drawing ever tighter around them, Joe and Ebenezer left Delmarva and headed south in the spring of 1826, and it appears that Jesse W. Cannon left with them or at about the same time.

Jesse W. and his sister, Mary, are commonly believed to have been Patty's children, but they may have been the offspring of Jesse Cannon's earlier marriage to Fanny Brown. Jesse W. was married to Britannia Johnson, Joe's and Ebenezer's sister, and Mary was Joe's wife. The women, along with Sallie Sheehee, Ebenezer's spouse, may have preceded the men south with their children.

Because we take our national network of law-enforcement agencies and their sophisticated identification and tracking technologies for granted today, we may find it difficult to comprehend how easy it was in 1826 to become someone else. The brothers simply dropped their surname, Johnson, and assumed another in its place. Joseph Moore Johnson became Joseph or Josephus Moore—an alias he had used previously—and Ebenezer F. Johnson became Ebenezer Fraser. Jesse Cannon, who was not actively being sought, apparently felt there was no compelling reason to obscure his identity.

It was not until the remains of a slave dealer and three children were discovered at Patty's former Delaware residence in the spring of 1829 and Cyrus James, a young man who had been raised by Patty, implicated the Johnsons and his former mistress in their murders, that authorities took further action against the once desperate gang. Patty was arrested and confined in the Sussex County Jail, where she died of poison, tradition claims, under mysterious and still undocumented circumstances the following month. Indictments against the absent brothers were never served.

In Easton, Maryland, on April 14, 1829, the *Republican Star* reported: "One of the persons charged with these murders [Patty Cannon] has been committed to jail, but the principal offender [referring to Joe Johnson] has removed to a distant State."

The *Chestertown* [Maryland] *Telegraph* and the *Delaware Gazette* both informed their readers that Joe Johnson was said to be residing at that time in Alabama, possibly because Philadelphia Mayor Joseph Watson had suggested in an 1826 letter that the gang was selling out and moving to that state.

As far as I can determine, specific information about Joe Johnson filtered back to Delmarva only twice after his exodus. Robert B.

Hazard reported in *The History of Seaford* that Jacob Wright, a former neighbor of Johnson, had seen the fugitive in New Orleans while Wright was on a trip to Louisiana to sell a cargo of slaves, and Major Allen, who was closely related to Wright, told Hazzard that Johnson had presented Wright with a fine gold watch, apparently to buy his silence. Secondly, in a letter dated May 22, 1837, and addressed to magazine editor William P. Brobson, John M. Clayton, Delaware attorney and judge, United States Senator and Secretary of State under President Zachary Taylor wrote: "Powell of Seaford told me he saw him [Johnson] about a year ago on the levee at N. Orleans & knew him, but did not expose him as Johnson said he passed under another name & was a judge of Probate in the territory of Arkansas & begged Powell not to mention any thing of him."

Texas Researchers Sharon Moore and Patricia Pigg, the latter distantly related to Johnson, have been searching for years to uncover evidence of the trail Joe followed after leaving Dorchester County in 1826. His surviving tracks are mostly in the form of property transactions and census records.

While Mayor Watson, newspapers and later gossip have all suggested that Joe relocated to Alabama or Arkansas, George Alfred Townsend, in his beloved historical novel *The Entailed Hat*, seems to be the only writer who knew that Florida had been Joe's actual destination.

Several scenarios of Joe's southward migration are preserved in oral traditions. One branch of the Moore family claims that Josephus Moore was the owner of a fleet of schooners and that his cargo—reputed to have been imports from the African coast—was declared contraband by Boson port authorities when he attempted to land in Massachusetts. So Josephus ordered his captains to Charleston, South Carolina, where he sold both cargo and vessels and moved farther south in search of a new life. Joe had, of course, owned a schooner with which he transported kidnapped African Americans from Delmarva's Nanticoke River to lives of slavery in the South.

Josephus Moore appears on the Florida Census of 1830, living in Centerville, Leon County. In addition to any land he may have received under Florida's Homestead Act, Joe purchased at least three tracts of property for cash.

Sharon Moore admits that she and Pat Pigg have not exhausted research possibilities in the Sunshine State, and we all suspect that further efforts could uncover additional evidence of Joe's activity there, but because county boundaries began to change in 1827 and lines were drawn and redrawn repeatedly, research in that region can be tedious.

Later census records from Texas inform us that at least three children had been born to Joe and Mary while they lived in Maryland: Margarette in 1815, Jesse C. in 1817, and Josephus S. in 1824, while Martin H. was added to the family in Florida.

Margarette married Larkin Bell in Florida in 1831. They lived for a while in Leon County before moving to Decator County, Georgia, where Margarette gave birth to her first child in 1832. Mary also bore a child that year, Martha Jane, and she too was born in Georgia. It appears that mother and daughter were pregnant at the same time and probably living together. Mary has not been found in any records beyond 1832 and may have died shortly after the birth of Martha Jane.

Apparently ready to pull up stakes, Joe registered his Florida properties in 1834. Deeds in those days were sometimes held as easily accessible collateral and recorded at the courthouse only when one was preparing to sell or otherwise transfer them. It is the last we hear of Joe's whereabouts until the New Orleans reports from Wright and Powell, when he was said to have informed Powell that he was a judge in Arkansas.

No concrete evidence has thus far been discovered to place Joe in Arkansas, but in 1838, his brother, Ebenezer, was living in the Pine Prairie District—now Little River County—in that newly admitted state. Nearby lived a man by the name of Larkin B. Moore. Remember the husband of Joe's daughter Margarette, whose name was Larkin Bell. We can only wonder if Larkin B. Moore may have been another Joe Johnson alias.

Joe's next clear track is discovered on a petition that he and

Ebenezer and their sister, Britannia, all signed in 1839, appealing for a new county [Harrison] to be formed in the Redlands of East Texas.

When Methodist minister and physician Job Baker arrived to spread the Gospel in 1839, the Redlands was a turbulent territory. "There was not a preacher of any kind in the county besides myself," Baker would later write in his memoirs. "I settled in the neighborhood of Mr. Page and Mr. Josephus Moore, men of unenviable reputation."

Between 1839 and 1844, a feud known as the Regulator-Moderator War raged between two groups in Northeast Texas. The roots of the conflict lay primarily in frauds and land swindling that had once been rife between the American and Mexican borders. Homes were burned, men were murdered, courts were intimidated and tempers ran hot until the outbreak of the Mexican War, when both sides amicably joined forces to fight a common enemy. Neighbors Moore and Page were affiliated with the Moderators.

To further complicate the lives of settlers, the Cherokee War broke out in 1839. Job Baker wrote in his memoirs: "We moved into Fort Crawford, and for months had not flour, meat, or coffee. We lived on corn pounded in a mortar."

Fifteen years afterward, in 1854, when legislation was passed to entitle veterans of the Indian War to apply for benefits, a claim on behalf of Joe's minor orphans was filed by Josephus S. Moore, Joe's son, suggesting his father's participation in the conflict, probably as a Texas Ranger.

The Texas Rangers had been initiated in 1824 by Stephen Austin when he hired ten frontiersmen to conduct a punitive expedition against a band of renegade Indians. Formally instituted by the Texas Legislature and expanded to three companies in 1835, the Rangers participated, to their chagrin, in very limited action during the Revolution. But in 1838, when Mirabeau Lamar succeeded to the presidency, the role of the Rangers changed drastically, and for the next three years they waged all-out war on the Indians, most notably in the Cherokee conflict and then against the Comanches two years afterward. Many Rangers were volunteers who supplied their own mount, weapons and accouterments, and it requires no great imagination to believe that Joe may have been one of them.

In January 1841, a year in which Josephus Moore appears on Harrison County records as justice of the peace, he married neighbor Mary Jane Page, David Page's daughter and a woman nearly half his age. Later that year, Mary Jane gave birth to their first child, John David Moore, who would lose his life fighting for the Confederacy near Richmond in the Civil War.

While records and family recollections differ on the date, it was about this time that a companion of David Page was killed by Indians. David was questioned by a company of Regulators from Red River County and found to be in possession of counterfeit money, which Moderators were known to be producing. He was charged with committing the murder, and in spite of an eloquent last-minute appeal by Senator Robert Potter, the Regulators lynched him without a trial.

Joe may first have been drawn to the Southwest when the United States and Mexico, unable to agree on a boundary, had established a fifty-mile-wide neutral ground between the two nations. After winning independence, Texas broadened the attraction to immigrants by offering free land.

To facilitate an expansion of its tax base, the new republic granted headrights to almost anyone making application, the only requirements being that the new owners had to survey the property and improve or occupy it within a specified period of time—usually three years. In addition, individuals could procure unclaimed land by simply surveying and registering it.

In spite of the generous policies which permitted Joe and his extended family to legally acquire large tracts of land in at least four Northeast Texas counties, the deposed Delmarva outlaw apparently could not resist twisting the rules. Sharon Moore and Pat Pigg were barely able to contain their amusement when they discovered the names of Cyrus James and Jimmy Phoebus on Texas survey maps. Cyrus James, you should recall, provided the testimony that resulted in multiple indictments of murder against Patty Cannon and the Johnson brothers, and Phoebus was a citizen of Princess Anne,

Maryland, who was later immortalized as a character in *The Entailed Hat*. There is no evidence that either man ever migrated to Texas or applied for land there, and after the named claimants failed to show, members of Joe's family annexed the real estate.

In the 1840s, a traveling commission began checking into the legitimacy of land applications and testaments, and some of the people to whom Joe had sold fraudulently acquired property found themselves with worthless titles. Suits were filed against him and court judgments won.

Perhaps on the run again, Joe apparently relocated several times during the last ten years of his life, leaving little documentation of his activities. In one item, a letter dated November 25, 1847, and postmarked at Crockett, Texas, Joe pleads with his daughter Margarette, still living in Georgia, to visit him and possibly settle there, informing her that he owned ample land for all of his children—a rarely recorded display of sentimentality from this hard and brutal man.

Joe's name does not appear in any form on the Texas Census Index in 1850, but close scrutiny of the tally sheets shows that he and his second family were living with his son Jesse in Leon County, where Joe was listed as overseer.

Sometime late in 1853, Joe left Leon County on a cattle drive with his mother-in-law, Jinnette Page, and her son Eligah. The small party was bound for Harrison County, where Joe's brother, Ebenezer, conducted business and where Jinnette owned ranchland. Joe's wife, Mary Jane, had died earlier in the year, leaving behind five young children.

As they camped near the present location of Kilgore, Texas, the small party was attacked by Indians. Jinnette escaped unharmed with her wounded son, but Joseph Moore Johnson, alias Josephus Moore, once the scourge of free African Americans from Philadelphia to Baltimore and the length and breath of Delmarva, was killed at the age of fifty-eight. Sixteen days later, his mother-in-law returned to the scene and buried the remains she found in an unmarked and now forgotten grave along the shallow, winding waterway named Rabbit Creek.

No Secrets between Us

Some readers may be shocked by this story, others will feel anger, and a few are certain to be upset with me for writing it. I have been offered considerable advice about how to present this small fragment of nearly forgotten Delmarva history, along with several strong admonishments to destroy the material and forget about it. It is offered because I believe that knowing and intelligently evaluating all of the past, not only that which pleases us or projects a favored image, is a necessary step in the process of advancing our society. Nothing reported here is intended by me or should ever be directed as an accusation against any person or community. It is simply a record of something that happened a long time ago, something that should remind us of how far we have progressed as well as how much we need to continue to strive for equality and under-standing.

At precisely nine o'clock on Monday evening, May 28, 1923, every town on Delmarva, I am told, conducted a simultaneous demonstration of unity. One of those exhibitions took place on the lot adjacent to the Manokin Presbyterian Church, a lovely, eighteenth century brick edifice that sits on a hill across the bridge from downtown Princess Anne. There, a huge cross had been erected, and as members of the Princess Anne Ku Klux Klan marched to the scene in full regalia, the symbol of Christ's crucifixion was set ablaze. With flames leaping into the night sky and the

Stars and Stripes fluttering in the evening breeze, Klansmen circled the cross and sang two stanzas of "America."

After standing silently for a few minutes in the flickering light, the hooded figures quietly reformed into line and marched back to their lodge. Observers called it a quiet and impressive demonstration, conducted with the cooperation of town authorities and witnessed by a large crowd.

Two days later the Princess Anne Klansmen journeyed to a quiet community on the Nanticoke River to participate in the largest event in that town's history. Singly and in caravans, automobiles and buses arrived in Sharptown throughout the day on Wednesday, May 30, until more than 2,000 had been directed by members of the State Motor Police into every available parking space.

"As if in answer to the critics and enemies of the Knights of the Ku Klux Klan," the *Marylander and Herald* reported, "over 10,000 people gathered at Sharptown...to witness and participate in one of the biggest public Naturalizations ever held in this part of the United States."

After supper was served by women of the Methodist Church, representatives from every Klan between Wilmington, Delaware, and Onancock, Virginia, formed in parade and filed to a ten-acre field at the edge of town, accompanied by a marching band and two, white-robed horses outlined in electric lights. Observers gathered on the grassy knoll, men in their best suits and hats, boys in knickers, jackets and caps, and ladies held their long dress coats closed against the evening chill.

The *Marylander and Herald* described the scene in these words: "When the thousands arrived in the field, it was found that the ten acres was a living mass of people attracted from every point on the Shore, and considerable work had to be done by the white-robed Klansmen to clear a space large enough to stage the Naturalization.

"A huge forty-foot cross had been erected on a hilltop in the field and soon could be seen for miles around, blazing forth the word that the Klan was firmly entrenched in this territory and here to stay, and telling in its bright lights that the Klan stood on the life of Christ and took that life as its criterion of character.

"With the assembling of over 200 candidates for admission into the mysteries of Klandom, the Princess Anne degree team, which had been selected to put on the Naturalization, started this band through the lines that led them into a greater realization of their duties as Americans, as citizens, and as men.

"With thousands of eyes watching the whole works, these men were admitted to the Ku Klux Klan, going through the necessary steps and taking the necessary obligations that made them then a part of that great body of men that is causing so much talk and criticism in the United States today.

"While the parade was made back of the so-called mask, as soon as the paraders reached the grounds, and from that time on, the visors were lifted, and they mingled among the crowd with their faces bared, so that all who desired could see their faces."

Following the "Naturalization," Dr. J. H. Hawkins delivered an address to the thousands present. He reviewed the declared principals of the Klan and asked the crowd to examine the men assembled in white robes and judge for themselves if the candidates were hoodlums and criminals.

"These men stand before you tonight with faces revealed," he said. "Do you see among them any criminals? Do you see any bootleggers? Do you see any violators of the laws of our country? No, you see the best manhood on this entire peninsula, men who are making sacrifices daily to live the lives of Klansmen, clean men who are willing to fight for what is right. They are your husbands, your fathers, your sons, and your sweethearts. Is there one among you tonight who is ashamed of these men in white?"

Cries of "No!" greeted the doctor's question.

An unnamed minister of the gospel, one of many Delmarva clergy reported to have been present, was quoted as saying: "I have heard and read much of the Ku Klux Klan, and I was attracted here tonight to get at first hand an impression of the character of men that formed this great organization. I have not seen any of the roughnecks, the criminals, the lawbreakers, the gamblers, nor the bootleggers or hoodlums here that the public press rave about, but have seen the cream of our citizenship, real men with grim faces and determination, rich men and poor men side by side fighting for a principal, and I know that the reports are untrue. An organization formed of the caliber of men that I saw tonight are not going to break any laws, they are not going to take any laws into their own hands, they are going to make, through proper channels—the channels of the law—our beloved Eastern Shore a better place to live and to raise our children. From the looks of grim determination on the faces of these men tonight, I got an inspiration, and I am willing to leave in the hands of these men the future of our country. I know they mean business, and that the lives of the lawbreakers, the criminals, the home breakers, the bootleggers, and all others who are not living clean upright lives are going to be hard ones from now henceforth. I was proud of these men in white tonight, and while I am not a member of their organization, I intend to be, and I pray God to strengthen them so they will not falter or fall by the wayside in the great fight that they have started."

To the credit of the town and the crowd, not a single accident or act of misconduct was reported by the press throughout the day and evening, and when the Naturalization and speeches ended, the crowds returned to their vehicles and quietly disappeared into the darkness.

The *Marylander and Herald* concluded its report of the incident with this paragraph: "The Peninsula, composed of the three counties of Delaware, the nine counties of Maryland and the two counties of Virginia, is now a network of Klan organizations. Every town of any size has a Klan, and the smaller ones are enrolled in the membership of their nearest neighbors. The fight is on here, and no one is saying 'let's turn back.'"

The first Klan in the United States originated in 1866 as a social club for young men in Pulaski, Tennessee. When their strange, unintelligible rituals and hooded white robes were observed to have a sobering effect on superstitious former slaves, the organization's objectives were quickly redirected to curbing activities of the emancipated black population.

In the summer of 1867 the Klan held its first formal meeting in Nashville, where it was organized into local "dens," and General

Nathan Forrest, the famous Confederate cavalry leader, was chosen as its president or Grand Cyclops.

Encouraged by this inaugural group's success, additional lodges organized and rapidly spread throughout the former Confederacy during 1867 and 1868. The original lodge along with the Knights of the White Camellia, the White League, the Invisible Circle and the Pale Faces all came to be collectively referred to as the Ku Klux Klan.

In their adopted declaration of principals, the following objectives were defined: (1) to protect the weak and to relieve the injured and oppressed, (2) to protect and defend the Constitution of the United States and laws passed in conformity thereto, and to protect the states and people from invasion from any source and (3) to aid in the execution of the laws and to protect the people from unlawful seizure and trial except by their peers.

In retrospect and reality, however, the objectives were clearly to protect the white population, to reduce the black vote, to expel the Northern carpetbaggers and scalawags and to nullify those laws of Congress that might place Southern whites under the control of a party largely supported by black voters. When most of these ends had been realized by 1877, the original Klan disbanded, leaving behind a scattered collection of local and mostly renegade groups.

Then, in 1915 at Stone Mountain, Georgia, William Joseph Simmons formed a fraternal organization devoted to the principles of white supremacy. It was an entirely new group but it adopted the name of the original Klan. By 1919, activities were being directed not only against blacks but also against Roman Catholics, Jews, and all foreign-born. The dedication of the organization was to protect the purity and values of native-born, white, Anglo-Saxon Americans. It claimed to serve a higher morality and a dedication to religious fundamentalism.

With its national rather than sectional appeal, the influence of the new Klan quickly spread beyond the boundaries of the old Confederacy, and at the height of its power in the early 1920s, between 4,000,000 and 6,000,000 Americans claimed membership. Many Klansmen were elected to political posts at the local level, and the

Klan contributed heavily to splitting the Democratic Convention in 1924.

National sentiment against the Klan began to grow as incidents of intimidation, whipping, tarring and feathering, branding, mutilating and lynching were publicized, and by the 1930s it again had dwindled to an ineffective organization, primarily scattered through the South.

The men who wore the white hoods on May 30, 1923, are gone. One old man who was there remembers the event only through the eyes and the mentality of the child he was in 1923. His older brother wore a hood that night, and his father sawed the timbers used to construct the forty-foot cross.

"It was a social thing," another octogenarian told me, perhaps naively. "They would have picnics and parties. Even the minister belonged to it. People came from two or three states around just to have fun."

"The Ku Klux Klan was strong here in the twenties," another said. "I bet there wasn't one out of fifty people in business that wasn't in it. I knew a whole lot of them, but they're all dead now. They were well-to-do people. There was a grand wizard lived in town. Some know his name, but they won't give it out to this day."

"There wasn't much law and order then," a woman added. "There were no cops here. The Ku Klux Klan was all they had. It helped to maintain order in town. The only thing I ever heard tell of them doing around here—a man beat his wife up, and two or three of them went to his home and told him he better not do it again. They were all dressed up in their white robes, and you know, that stopped it. They didn't have no trouble, didn't bother nobody. It was more like a vigilante group to keep men in line—not racist."

But there are recollections of racism. Another woman remembers an old newspaper report of an Independence Day celebration that included a description of one of the activities: "They painted a ball black and put a face on it. The big game was getting to hit that ball."

And an elderly black woman shared this seventy-eight-year-old memory: "We seen that fire in the sky, and all them white people come to town. There was talk of trouble and Momma didn't let me go to work the next day. We didn't know what to think. I worked for Miss Mary then. Miss Mary sent her boy over to see why I didn't come. He said, 'No trouble,' so I went with him. They were nice folks. They were good to my Momma and me. But one man had trouble in town one time. He went over there in the nighttime. It was O.K to go to work or to the store in the daytime, but you didn't go there at nighttime. No sir, you never done that—not in them days.

There is, of course, much more to the story than is evident in the biased words of one newspaper reporter and the misty recollections of a few elderly citizens. The human mind is often unconsciously selective of what it remembers, and it does not always empower us to admit all that we know. In the process of researching and preparing this narrative, I have been reminded that a society is only as sick as its secrets. Let there be no secrets between us.

"Naturalization" at Sharptown,

Maryland—May 30, 1923

Coming of the Bridge

During the nearly two centuries of domination by Great Britain, the Chesapeake Bay offered tidewater Marylanders a facility of contact with one another and with the outside world that was unique among the thirteen colonies, but as our population grew, it spread inland, and the bay gradually became a barrier rather than a bond between the Eastern Shore and the rest of Maryland.

Until 1952 the only way a traveler from the west or south could directly reach the Eastern Shore of the Chesapeake was by water, and for more than a hundred and fifty years—until steamboats began to ply the bay on regularly scheduled runs—power to make the crossing was provided by wind filling a cloth sail. The only other way to get there was a roundabout journey on narrow, often muddy trails through Cecil County at the head of the bay.

By 1911, with an increase in automobile ownership and the accompanying yen to travel, a seventeen-year-old, side-loading steam excursion boat was re-christened the *Governor Emerson C. Harrington* by a private company, and Maryland's first regularly scheduled Chesapeake Bay ferry was initiated. The twenty-three-mile trip between Annapolis and the railhead at Claiborne consumed two hours.

But other ideas about getting from one shore to the other were beginning to ferment. Three years earlier, in 1908, State Senator Peter C. Campbell observed that railways running out of the Eastern Shore were carrying the majority of Shore trade north to Wilmington and Philadelphia. He suggested a bridge be constructed to provide a direct route to Baltimore. Impressed by his arguments, city merchants and manufacturers allotted $1,000 for an engineering survey to determine the feasibility of constructing a bridge to extend interurban trolley lines across the estuary from Bay Shore to Tolchester. When the study committee announced that the cost of such a bridge would be $13,000,000, the project was placed on hold.

Private interests were finally organized in 1926 and granted state and federal authorization to raise funds to build a bridge between Miller Island and Tolchester. Money began to trickle in slowly, but the 1929 financial crash put an end to the project.

Efforts to improve ferry service resulted in a new terminal at Matapeake in 1930, reducing the crossing from 23 to 8.7 miles, although trips to Claiborne continued on a lighter schedule. The *Governor Albert C. Ritchie* and the *John M. Dennis*, both double-end, diesel ferryboats, were then making daily runs back and forth across the bay.

In 1937, the Maryland General Assembly directed the State Roads Commission to draw up a comprehensive plan for the construction of bridges and tunnels and authorized the issuance of revenue bonds—payable through collection of tolls—to cover costs of construction. The Susquehanna and Potomac River bridges were completed under this act, but World War II delayed the third and largest project, a bay crossing.

1937 was a landmark year for another reason. To avoid navigational hazards in the Baltimore area and to tie in with north-south and east-west highways, the site for the bridge was shifted from Bay Shore-Tolchester to Sandy Point-Matapeake. Sandy Point also became the ferry's western terminal during World War II, when the State Roads Commission took over the Chesapeake Bay Ferry System and moved it from the narrow streets of downtown Annapolis.

It was Governor William Preston Lane, Jr., in 1947, who proposed an expansion of the Acts of 1937 to direct specifically that a Chesapeake Bay span be built, and the Maryland General Assembly passed the necessary legislation.

Construction began in January 1949 as bulldozers began to prepare a site for the western approach to the bridge, but before over-water work could commence, the state had to win a court battle with tunnel advocates. Once that last-minute hurdle was out of the way, dredges began the three-month task of digging a new ferry channel on November 3. The old channel had to be moved because it crossed the proposed bridge line.

In 1950, the largest marine construction flotilla ever assembled on the East Coast came together off Sandy Point, including more than 100 dredges, huge floating cranes, mammoth pile drivers, floating construction docks and boats and barges of every description. The first permanent piles were driven in March, and by year's end the major underwater tasks—the main tower and anchor piers —had been completed. Like an iceberg, much of the bridge lies beneath the surface, and one dollar out of every two spent on its construction went for underwater work.

One of the stumbling blocks to early plans for a bay crossing had been the high cost of deep-water foundations. This problem was solved during the construction of the Potomac River Bridge, when a new technique for constructing deep-water piers was developed that side-stepped the laborious and expensive creation of coffer-dams— watertight, below-surface enclosures that were pumped dry to permit work.

Every aspect of the construction had to be accomplished with pinpoint accuracy. Wooden surveyor's platforms, known as "dolphins," were built 200 feet from the centerline of each of the 26 piers. In the exact center of each dolphin, engineers drove a tack with a head one-eighth of an inch in diameter, and the tons of steel and concrete subsequently put underwater were controlled from the center of these tacks.

To construct the pier, a prefabricated wood platform with holes in it to receive the steel piles was lowered to the bottom and secured in precise vertical and horizontal alignment. The biggest pile drivers in existence were then used to drive the piles through the ooze, mud and clay into the firm stands underlying the bay. A case history was kept of each of the 4,130 piles driven, literally a blow-by-blow record to insure that every pile was sunk in the proper place with an accuracy, records claim, of one thirty-second of an inch, and every smash by the driver was controlled from the dolphins and checked by gyro-instruments.

Underwater carpenters then built up the sides of the sunken platforms to receive the concrete and complete the piers. Baltimore water was selected for the mix after a series of tests, and more than 4,000,000 gallons were hauled down the bay from the city to prepare the thousands of tons of cement and gravel for pouring.

Because the bridge is more than four miles in length, the curvature of the earth was one of many factors that engineers had to take into consideration. Due to the curvature, if you draw a straight line between points on opposite shores, you will discover that the water in the middle of the bay stands two and one half feet higher than at either shore, and the centerlines of two piers, constructed at right angles to the earth, gradually grow further apart as they extend upward.

The bridge also lengthens and shortens respectively with increases and decreases in temperature. Steel expands or contracts one-eighth of an inch per 100 feet each time the thermometer fluctuates 15 degrees. On the day I wrote these words, the 22,900-foot-long span grew five feet in length between the hours of 5:00 a.m. and 3:00 p.m. Expansion joints and the use of rivets rather than welding absorb such changes. Nearly 5,000,000 rivets were employed in fabricating the steel parts.

Winds sweeping over and under the 1,600-foot-long suspension span present yet another problem by creating lift, much as they do on an airplane wing. To break the vacuum effect, on which wing lift depends, vents were incorporated into the center span's floor.

The first topside steel, a unit 300 feet in length, was floated in place atop its piers in January 1951, and sixteen months later

May 1952, the final superstructure element, a 400-ton section, was raised from the surface of the bay into place on the east end of the suspension span. Maryland's Eastern and Western shores had finally been joined by what was then the third longest bridge in the world.

But the job had not proceeded without its setbacks. Two onslaughts of high wind and rough water that struck almost a year apart caused major headaches for builders. In November 1950, winds of hurricane force blew away a barge loaded with 600 steel piles for the east anchor pier. After a three-week search, a United States Coast and Geodetic Survey plane carrying a magnetic device located the sunken vessel. It was resting beneath 30 feet of water, six miles northeast of the bridge site. An Army Corps of Engineers' boat furnished with sound-echo equipment pinpointed the location and the piles were retrieved.

Then, in December 1951, a 480-foot, 1,500-ton span, rising 130 feet above the water, broke loose while being towed and ran hard aground on Kent Island. The span had to be partially dismantled, towed back to the erection dock, reassembled, and then start its journey to the bridge again.

In the same year, Governor McKeldin became concerned about rumors of faulty design and deficiencies in the bridge structure and sked that an inquiry be conducted. While no major flaws were tected, some design changes were made on the Eastern Shore seway, which was found to be vulnerable to ice and waves.

Vednesday, July 30, 1952, was a nearly perfect summer day for 'ge dedication, and a crowd of 10,000 enthusiastic observers out for the occasion. Governor McKeldin's arrival was greet- 'iineteen-gun salute, and ceremonies got underway at 10:40 by side, former Governor Lane and Governor McKeldin cut 's to open the span.

units from all the services paid tribute to officials on the nd, and former senator George Radcliffe, chairman of committee, began to introduce a parade of speakers 'lmost three hours of steady oratory. The principal ernor Lane, who had brought the dream of a bridge to reality and in whose honor the twin spans are named today. He urged that it be called "The Memorial Bridge" in reverence to Maryland's dead in WW II.

Governor McKeldin called for resistance to the onslaught of "hot-dog venders and billboard raisers" expected to beset the new highways leading to the bridge. "There will be a tendency to commercialize where there is no proper place for commercialization," he warned. "There will be a temptation to cheapen the roadsides for personal gain. Such cheap commercialism mars the beauty of the state and adds dangers to driving by adding sharp cutoffs to the highways and obstructing motoring vision. I promise you now that the state government will do all in its power to prevent such undesirable development, and I urge the authorities of the counties on each side of the bridge and along all the approaching roads to see that their zoning is strong enough and effective enough to keep these areas scenic places, which we can be proud to show our visitors and which we ourselves can enjoy."

After ceremonies on the western side were completed, officials began the first crossing of the bridge, taking one hour and fifteen minutes to cover the four miles, with numerous stops for the benefit of press, television, movie and magazine cameramen. While the caravan crept along, one of the old ferryboats, on its last day of operation, made four shore-to-shore trips.

On the Eastern side, duplicate ceremonies dragged on toward 5:00 p.m., until, much to the crowd's appreciation, an amplifier problem cut the speeches short. The real centers of attention for those who stood for hours in the sweltering, 90-degree heat were the bridge itself, the motorcade of old cars, the flotilla of yachts on the bay, the planes buzzing overhead—one displaying a large banner reading: "The Bay Bridge Leads to Ocean City"—and the numerous sandwich and soda stands.

As a late afternoon ferry made its last run between the slips at Sandy Point and Matapeake, a fleet of buses carried people back and forth over the new span free of charge. Then, at 6:01 p.m., the Chesapeake Bay Bridge officially opened to toll traffic, and attendants in five toll booths began to collect $1.40 per car and driver traveling in either direction, plus 25¢ for each passenger.

On Friday, August 1, the following editorial appeared in East-on's *Star Democrat*:

"The saying, 'Never the twain shall meet,' may hold true for continents, but as for the Eastern Shore and the Western Shore of Maryland, they have now definitely met with the opening, Wednesday, of the Bay Bridge across the Chesapeake Bay.

"In the entire history of the Free State, the Eastern Shore has been considered a separate section of Maryland. Rich in heritage and quaint customs, the 'Sho has always stood apart from the rest of the State of Maryland and the Nation as a distinct area of proud independence. Friction grew so great in one section of Maryland's history that the Eastern Shore counties tried to join the three counties of the State of Delaware—not once but FIVE different times.

"In the last century of the Shore's history, no steps have been tried to join the neighboring state, but political bitterness between legislators from the Eastern Shore and the Baltimore politicians has continued into the present time.

"This bitterness has led the Western Shore into a look-down-the-nose attitude toward the 'backwoods people' on the Eastern Shore. In the past, we, here on the Eastern Shore, have been considered political slaves of the wishes of Baltimore politicians.

"Not helping the situation in any way, has been the past attitude of the Baltimore and Washington papers. They have ignored the news and features of the Eastern Shore and have contained their pages to metropolitan news.

"This picture has now suddenly changed with the opening of the Bay Bridge. Now, they are fighting tooth and nail for stories about the Shore in an effort to gain the love and circulation of the Eastern Shore. Why? For now they feel the Bridge will open an easy avenue across the Chesapeake to the stores of Baltimore and Washington. For now the 'backwoods people' are going to throw away their wish books of the mail-order houses and come to the big city to buy their store clothes.

"Part of this will be true, but it will also work in reverse. Many people from the Western Shore will soon make their first visit to the Eastern Shore and find—many to their amazement—that we have modern stores, modern plumbing, and wear shoes. They will also find that life is not too slow over here and that it is certainly a lot more pleasant than in the city.

"But even more important, it is hoped that the new span of concrete and steel will cement the East and West together into a team that will strengthen Maryland as a state, free from false ideas of grandeur, on one side, and the feeling of oppression on the other.

"Yes, a new era of transportation has now been opened, which will also open the eyes of many—from both sides of the tracks"

When I called Anne Arundel County "home," I considered the new bridge to be one of the greatest blessings in my life. It permitted me to quickly escape the congestion of the Western Shore and the responsibilities of what was often a 60-hour-a-week job. But now that I am a full-time, Eastern Shore "come here,' I often wish, like many elderly, nostalgic "from heres," that it would go away.